When Bree Durning's ovarian cancer reoccurs, everything she and husband Will believed about their life together is upended and Bree finds herself heading down a path that Will cannot follow, or even understand. Michele Merens has given us a sensitive and beautifully rendered portrait of a marriage in extremis.
  ~ Yona Zeldis McDonough, Fiction Editor, *Lilith Magazine*

Inside Our Days is a deep dive into family history, memory, trauma and care that swept me up and carried me…I read this book in two breathless days then looked up, blinking, to find myself delivered back into my own life. Michele Merens knows something about how memory and love both can morph, twist, slip away from us and come back again changed and still present. And the strength and courage it takes to continue to choose to walk out into the world, one day at a time.
  ~ Sarah Sadie, author of *We Are Traveling Through Dark at Tremendous Speeds*

Michele Merens has written a beautifully tender novel about the ways sick people sometimes hurt the ones they love. However, it is also a novel that probes, with raw, unflinching courage, how the selflessness of the living, who come like supplicants confused and full of need, can become selfishness to those dying slowly. In the end, though we know none return from the dark shore, we are left with the notion that one must, like a magpie, "build a universe out of whatever is small and precious and catches your eye."
  ~ Carlo Matos, author of *The Quitters*

1

Inside Our Days

Inside Our Days

~Michele Merens~

First Edition
Paperback ISBN: 978-0-578-70758-7

Cover Design by Adrian Gonzalez and Tom Wallestad
Interior design and typesetting by Keegan Berry, Adrian Gonzalez, and Courtney Makinen

Muriel Press
Marian University Wisconsin
45 S. National Ave,
Fond du Lac, WI 54935
murielpress@marianuniversity.edu

Inside Our Days is a work of fiction, and as such, all characters, names, events, and locales are products of the author's imagination. Any resemblance to real events or people, living or dead, is purely coincidental. While the author, editors, and publisher have worked to describe a variety of mental and physical disorders with accuracy, none of these parties are responsible for any errors, misrepresentations, or omissions describing diagnoses, symptoms, or treatment put forth for any illnesses represented or implied. Furthermore, readers are urged not to rely on any information put forth in this story for self-diagnosis or self-treatment of any condition but encouraged to consult with a medical professional.

This novel is dedicated to the late author Joy (B.J.) Chute with unending appreciation for her wise mentoring and generous heart, and with so much love for friends and family, especially Ben and Hope.

Part One

~ 1 ~

The argument of our lives turns out not to be with God or other people: against their politics or worldviews versus our own. It seems to William the argument of life ultimately comes down to no more than one main contention: an argument against *that day.*

That day, or for some that night. For none of us can escape the reality that on some unknown day or night, our lives will end. He knows people who have had a brief glimpse of their last day earlier than others. They've suffered traumas that have made the rest of their time on this earth, however long, gloomier and bigger than all that has come before. These people are his patients. He talks with them in the abstract about death every day. "Oh doctor, I want to die." "I'm afraid of life as it is now." At least once a week, usually more, he tackles the subject in depth and not in the abstract, leading clients through the extreme notion of the world without them in it like Capra's fine movie, or someone's pastor offering up a eulogy. He urges them to think of their best selves in such scenarios so they'll have something to hang onto, be proud of, even if he is only inventing as he goes along.

Nonetheless, Bree is again facing the reality of that day with no reprieve, and William cannot be sure how either of them will resolve these arguments now.

The night before had been punctuated with the normal spate of bad weather predictions on the news and Bree trying to be normal too, mostly because she was so exhausted with being otherwise. Last night she'd been quiet, demanding thoughts and space of her own. Rubbing the last vestiges of hand cream across her elbows, pushing over to the farthest corners of the bed to be away from his reach. The blankets moved with her and far from him, same as a low-pulling tide.

To such assaults, William is only mildly indignant. For even without her, he can claim an open book as some kind of protection against promised insomnia. Of course, he knows this joint pretense at any normalcy will fail, that in the morning with sleep or without, they will both come up from their exhaustion to receive all the world's bad news.

But does that mean each morning and for every morning until her final days, he is doomed to fail her? Or will they both fail each other by not speaking more of this returning diagnosis? Will each night spent pretending to read books or holding hands in the newly grim dark devolve not only into moments lost but utter failures of nerve?

In the morning, the phone rings before six; it is a call routed by the service from a patient who cannot handle his own anxiety, whose mind has crawled along so many corridors all night that now he feels like a rat, just as feral and small-boned. After William talks with him for ten minutes or so, schedules him in for an emergency hour at four, he feels dirty himself and tries to crawl back into bed for quick repairs. But suddenly he is crying with such desperation he leans up against Bree, spoons her, until she lets him in.

Afterwards, William comes into the bathroom, only able to mumble, "Sorry, sorry." This is his new posture with her since they'd heard from her oncologist weeks ago.

She turns around, the toothbrush poking up in her mouth. Is she worn out by the way he'd approached her this morning? Resentful? She won't tell. Her blond-grey curls seem thin up along the brow and no signs of red off the cheeks or chin; just minty white paste.

"Sorry about," he starts then regroups, "that call before the alarm went off."

"A hospitalization?"

"No, just a new patient. Testing me probably. Don't worry." He dares another look, but she has bowed her head over the sink to spit. "I'm going to tell the service to not let those early calls through. We'll need sleep whenever we can get it."

"It's not the service that pissed me off," she says, turning. "It was when you came to me afterwards."

He smiles. "That's me being a selfish pig, right? I should've asked."

"That's not it. I was—glad."

"Oh? Well, whatever you want. From here on out, you just tell me. I don't want to hurt you. This morning I wasn't careful, I'll admit."

But she is beyond tired with his apologies, slams a wrist on the counter to let him know.

"Shut up, why can't you?" she shouts. "Stop making me say yes or no about everything! Like I know what's going on any better than you do. Sleep's what I wanted most! So why couldn't you just have started your day when the call came?"

Bree looks and sounds so childish with the toothbrush dangling, all her words garbled, and suddenly his guilt grows beyond reasonable bounds. Although William knows better, he feels like he's done something terribly wrong, He's molested a strange girl in bed only moments ago, not his wife of so many years.

This isn't a feeling to take on with everything else, so he doesn't. He shakes off the strangeness of the moment even as she moves back to the mirror and accuses, "So don't blame the service or anyone else for getting me up. When you were the one."

She is going to die. For the second time in three years, they've heard this truth from the doctor she trusts most, Bree's odds have shrunk even as the ovarian cancer's reconstituted, grown. Shorthand, these words for a simple equation: Bree's going to die sooner than we were thinking fourteen months ago when all the scans were coming back clean. But we're sure now, we're sure. So now the future's all a subtraction and the rest of our lives less, not more.

Out the window, the snowstorm has carved the backyard into curved surfaces and bulges unknown; piles of snow lean into each other much like Bree's cake bowls stacked in the pantry. Scents too, informing visitors to the kitchen of Bree's past triumphs; the fang-toothed smells from the spice cabinet; the clouds of cinnamon sugar on pastries; how she knows to stiffen the cream in donuts so that their insides are as kissable as she; how her chocolate Swiss rolls are so smooth they look like newly paved highways to his eye. But for the last five years in this home sugar has been poison, sugar feeds cancer. So, all those wonderful desserts now memories and this kitchen reconfigured as spare and sterile as a laboratory.

William boils water for coffee, guided by the glow of the stove rings. He prefers going through these daily routines in the near-dark hours before dawn. For even unlit, the house makes him feel safe in its shabby splendor.

15

In this home, William has always been able to create routines to find comfort. Decades of uninterrupted living here; the oversized pantry lost a foot of space to a double sink merely twelve years ago. The kitchen itself is so poorly upgraded they still push about the dishwasher on wheels from sink to garbage and back again each night, like some begging dog underfoot. And never mind that their two grown children have each offered to pay for renovations, never mind. "You can do it after we're gone then recoup your profits selling it all," he'd scoffed, refusing their offers. Now of course, those remarks only make him wince.

But safe, safe in this house for over two decades; they learned to ignore the yellowing patch of ceiling in the living room that warns of something rumbling through the bathroom pipes. Some clog of unknown origin and both of them Chicken Littles glancing up each morning for a falling patch of sky. Safe, for a half acre of yard in a prospering New York suburb nonetheless proved an ideal place for raising children and tending fickle gardens. Protected for nearly a century from vandals, speculators, flippers, and condo boards, this house has always survived.

"Survival once again the game," he mutters as he flips the stove dial to ON. Time to let everything regroup around that word.

~2~

"Mrs. Durning, how are we doing today?"

Bree manages a weak smile. Nurse Sabina clangs the scale as she pushes forward, then backward, to record any weight loss.

"I'm fine, thank you. And you?"

"Excited the weekend's coming. Time to recline, please."

The treatment bed, Bree knows it intimately. The faded black and grey padding, the cushioned small burp as she slides back, those seven tucks along its tightly braided seams.

The nurse dons her gloves.

"So Bree. How have you been feeling since last time? Your nausea?"

"Not so bad."

"On a scale of one to five, five the worst?"

She mumbles something about only a few incidents in the bathroom and maybe her expression draws pity. Nurse Sabina reassures as she opens a bottle of rubbing alcohol. From a container, she pulls a swab and draws near. Inhaling, Bree thinks of those peppermint stick jars on the fudge store counter during Cape May summers; *think Cape May*. And turn away from alcohol smells on those swabs; hold your breath so as not to inhale. Concentrate instead on the wet, cooling sensations of your skin being cleaned. Of you, fresh and new.

With brisk motions, the nurse adjusts her needled dose to her arm so the drugs will flow via tubes and a port previously laid under skin; a multi-channeled network of highways, bridges, and off ramps her doctors have crafted for alternating IV/IP treatments. Today, a simple outpatient procedure, and Bree's not quite sure why this usually friendly woman is so impatient. But as a doctor's wife she knows nurses shouldn't show their irritation, ever, around patients dragged down by their inescapable fatigue.

William is sitting in the waiting room just outside. For a split second, Bree's tempted to invite him in. If Sabina knows her husband's nearby, she'll surely play her part with good cheer.

On the other hand, her husband has a bad habit of touching everything he shouldn't when he's nervous. He pulls instruments from their cords, peers intensely at their assembly. The last time William sat with her, he'd nearly driven her and the nurses mad.

Sabina warns. "Don't fall asleep on me now."

Bree tenses but then gets the joke. Perhaps Nurse Sabina's care has been a bit erratic today. Nonetheless, this is still the woman who squats to slip her feet into warm socks, cups one of her heels like Prince Charming himself. Before Bree can even thank her for such courtesies, she is up again, swabbing skin with a sterilized pad. She is nothing if not efficient: *Bree, be grateful.*

The nurse adjusts her IV tube, gives Bree more space. Both of them seem to relax in the move.

"Now I'll be right in the next room if you need me."

She covers with a blue blanket and Bree closes her eyes. Settles back in darkness where Sabina and follow-up visits and sucking ports might fall away. Just lie back and allow the mind to take off, fly.

Yet, yet…something is failing her now. Where is the metronome in her head that starts up a rhythm and doesn't wind down but instead moves steadily upwards towards that comforting launch, *no more?*

Instead, Bree feels herself tensing from jaw to wrist. The diamond patterns in the carpet blur into oily spots. The smell of disinfectant threatens to gag. And behind closed lids? Blackness is blackness. Thoughts give way to anger with William, Nurse Sabina, others who have provoked today if only by their presence. She's been annoyed with them all. Why? Is it just this feeling of everyone claiming her body, her diagnosis, as their business? People get sick, and the world piles on.

And then…Bree isn't simply lying here, pinned down by needles and tubes. No.

Instead, she is back in her parent's decades-ago home where her own mother lay in bed after a car accident for nearly two years. That house was always filled with people they hardly knew; acquaintances from the neighborhood, the Parish, the Lion's Club, St. Agnes School. Over the same period, aunts, uncles, troops of nurses came to stay. Also, the women who did the laundry, scrubbed floors, they stayed. "God," their father would murmur as he polished his shoes at the kitchen table, "thank you for all these gals the church sends by."

All these strangers pouring in, so chores, homework, could always be put aside. And of course, there had to be "Thank you" for kindnesses, and "Please, come on in." No one was ever turned away, especially if they brought a sweet-smelling bag of groceries or clean linens. As far as

Bree's five-year-old self could see, some kind of party was always being held where everyone was having a grand, noisy time. Except for her mother, of course, who lay in a bedroom closest to the kitchen.

In that room, it was always quiet, quiet.

Even when people came to visit, they usually didn't cross the threshold to whisper their hellos. They'd look at the nurse sitting there as if she was a bathroom attendant expecting a tip, then finish up quickly to avoid conversations with any woman in uniform. A water glass sitting on a nightstand was always full, but mostly from melting ice chips; a dozen pill canisters lined up alongside. Frenzy only crept in occasionally, when lace-bullet patterns in the curtains battled sunbeams trying to push through.

For twenty months, their mother had been confined. Little else in the way of repairs existed then for broken limbs or hips except a hoisted rest. Pulleys had been installed over the bed so Bree could see between hanging sheets of canvas glimpses of her mother peeking through. The slings were prickly to the touch like fish scales and her mother's head was bandaged in such a way it seemed she wore a bathing cap to bed. Bree imagined she had a rubber-headed mom.

Back then her mother simply couldn't be approached unless some adult was kind and strong enough to lift five-year-old Bree so she could peer into a nest of crinkled pillows and sheets. There she lay, fragile as a doll wrapped in tissue paper, not to be touched. Yet even as her daughter leaned in for a good night's kiss, she would smell breath so fresh but how? She'd asked Eileen who'd simply snorted, "What do you think? The nurses give her dinner mints so she'll smell clean."

Bree had been duly impressed by this news. Her mother's sugared breath stood in stark contrast to Nurse Allie, who drank too much coffee and showed her black gums like a horse. Why didn't she sneak a mint now and then to keep herself nice? All the other tantalizing details of her mother's illness—such as the humidifier churnings that heaved up against Bree's bedroom walls like a kettle coming to a boil—seemed to recede luxuriously whenever Bree thought of her mother sucking on mints in her own defiant violation of the no candy rule in bed. So that's how people got past their pain, Bree decided. To get their strength back, their walks and hugs back, they needed candy to start.

Only years later did Bree stumble on another image of her mother to bracket the first. At a restaurant in France where diners could dagger their kill with merely manicured fingernails and a nod, she had gazed with wonder on a baby octopus suctioned along a glass tank wall. She'd recognized in its pale red shading glimpses of her mother's shaved scalp peeking out from wrapped gauze; heard in the steady rhythms of the tank's filter, the swoosh, swooshing of that humidifier. All these sights and sounds came together once again in a most startling way and yes, her mother was that creature's kin.

"How are you?"

"What?" Coming up from a doze, blinking at William, *who are you?*

"What can you stand?" he is saying to her. "Some juice? Or are you feeling too queasy?"

"Don't fuss," she grouses then pushes up on a sofa cushion. Still, he offers her cranberry juice in a glass along with a red and white striped straw. The straw stains purple as she sips, bubbles hiss her way.

He takes the glass from her only when it is empty and places it on a table alongside. "Better?"

"No. Weren't you listening when we got home? I asked you not to wake me."

Bree closes her eyes, but he's not obliging. He's still close enough for her to hear, "I'm sorry. I just thought you might want something cool to drink after a tough session." In fact, she can barely stand the way William's hovering near. Yet she's reluctant to say so, knowing her husband is simply working off the scripts of her prior illness, employing all the old step-and-fetch routines she wants to forget.

"I'm sorry too," she manages. "That I made you sit in the waiting room. But I really needed to go in by myself today."

William frowns but then surprises her by not asking why this session was different than any other.

"I don't mind sitting outside," he says instead. "I'm happy to wait. Look, my appointments can always be rescheduled. We might as well take advantage of the times I can get away, huh?"

"I told you that's not necessary. Carla and I can handle my visits to the clinic."

She can see he is hurt. She's not only rejecting him as a medical professional with the wrong expertise, but also as a husband who can no longer please his wife with juice breaks or massages or even a reassuring presence.

Bree tries to sit up, her blanket shifts in the move. William's disciplined enough to resist rearranging the fold, but he does pick up her straw and start beating it along the edge of the coffee table.

"All the ways we can rethink our daily routines. That's what family leave is for," he repeats sourly.

"There's no point. You'd be redundant. Carla knows what I need."

No, she doesn't like hearing herself sound the shrew. She blames chemo; oh, she blames it so much. Her doctor has said treatment at this stage can push off intolerable pains and maybe, just maybe, extend her life for months longer than without. Yet she's been attacking William when the nausea comes up so quick and hard afterwards and how much misery is he expected to bear?

"Will you start to listen, William? Because I've got sort of an announcement," she says, inhaling to boost her courage. "And you know, it's not open to debate. All right?"

William starts to protest then stops himself. Playing along.

"The chemo," she tells him. "I'm thinking—well, I'm thinking I want to stop."

Still holding the straw her husband swipes at the air. "I'm sure recurrence brings up all the old fears again."

"I'm not afraid, that's not what this is all about," Bree counters. "As far as cutting off chemo, Dr. Sands told us this time treatment can be palliative after a certain point, right? But still, I signed on. And I've done a round now and—."

"Chemo can buy you months," he interrupts, perhaps moving in too fast. "You're not really making sense, Bree. When we talked with Sands, I got the impression you wanted an aggressive treatment plan. You pushed to have the port put back in."

"And now I want them to take it out."

"Who knows when that could get scheduled?"

"So let's ask," she retorts, knowing he's stalling and not in the mood to hear. "I'll go through that procedure again as soon as they offer it, sure. Then you'll know I'm serious."

William's jaw twitches and she can guess why; he hates it when conversations detour into places where he's not sure how to circle back.

"If it's been too hard on you this month, perhaps we could tell them to pull back. Maybe you can look at something new, a clinical trial?"

A compromise yet Bree can only shake her head back and forth, no.

He registers this, shifts his glance to the table. It's clear a wet spot from her glass on the wood is bothering him but he won't lean over to make repairs.

"See how you're feeling in a few days. If you can consider two more rounds, three tops, that's all I ask. Then you have a break anyway, and I promise we'll both take a good, hard look at our options. I want to respect you here Bree—it's just. I mean, we're still trusting Sands, aren't we?"

"Of course, I trust him. But we're not talking remission this time. He's not offering me years."

"No one can know with absolute—."

"Please."

"This isn't something we need to figure out now," he mutters.

"But we do! Aren't you listening to me?"

"Yes."

Unable to help herself she continues, "You know what I don't need to talk about? Whether or not I wanted to wake up for juice. Do you hear?"

24

~3~

"Claire! Eileen!"

Their fingers touching, knotting.

"So you are—greyer."

"Let's just go on about the grey."

"William?"

Bree's glance flicks his way then retreats.

Only a few minutes ago, her two sisters had climbed out of the airport limo, presented themselves at their door. They have come into their home with reddened eyes, tissues rolled into sleeves, so he knows there's been some serious commiserating beforehand. With Bree, though, they will only offer up wisecracks, the usual banter delivered up in Jersey accents of long rs and fudged ds.

As usual, Eileen's face is set with worry and reminds William of his father-in-law. The younger two have escaped this inheritance so far. The quality that pronounces itself most prominently in all three, however, has always been their height. Any time William has seen the Overton girls together, he never fails to notice. At 5'8", his wife always stands tall among groups of other women at parties or charity functions; nonetheless, she surrenders completely in size and coloring to the formidable Eileen. With their heights mimicking their birth order, Bree is in the middle in this trio. Eileen, as auburn as Bree waxes blonde, stands inches taller. Claire is the smallest and least imposing of the three; yet her reddish-brown hair is the tornadic assault that sets her apart in any crowd.

Now arms circle each other, wrap as one. The Overton girls are in a team huddle and he is only the water boy. William picks up one of Eileen's bags and as Bree pulls away from her sisters' embraces, she sees what he's doing. She thanks him by laying a hand on his arm. Her palm feels surprisingly warm, as if wired with excitement, energy.

"You're good to go," she whispers.

William is not quite sure what she means. Does she want him to disappear altogether? Eileen and Claire have already moved into the den draping coats and scarves in their wake, so this would be a good bet. The house is also transforming in ways he cannot control. Long silences normally mark their time together, the clatter of William's fingers on a laptop while Bree dozes on the burgundy couch. These sisters, however; they're chatter. Especially Claire, who's just arrived from a house filled with her own teenage girls.

"As much as you could expect," he hears Claire remark to her sisters as he heads into the hall.

"You're just jealous. We're past that stage," Bree counters.

"Stuck with the kiddies still, that's me, right."

"But that's exactly why I called you both. So we can get out of our funks."

"Eileen wants to kidnap you too, Bree," Claire volunteers.

"That's right," Eileen chimes in, all business and ready to make a proposition. "We talked in the cab about spending a few nights in a hotel."

As he listens, William can hear Bree's as surprised as he by this news, "You're not staying here? Why did you bring in your luggage?"

26

"That was a running debate we didn't quite resolve."

"Sure, we did," Eileen says. "On the way here, we checked out a Marriott and it looks wonderful. We're thinking you and William could come out to dinner with us. Then we'll check in. Tomorrow morning, we can make our plans for the rest of the week. You can stay with us and William can come pick you up for your doctor's appointment. Or maybe Claire and I could get you there. We'll figure it out."

"We're fine heading out to the Marriott for dinner," Bree replies. "But,"

William leans in, anxious to hear what his wife might say next.

"But also, my chemo's not part of our plan anymore," Bree announces. "That's over. I'm cutting off treatment."

Hearing her speak the words to others makes it real, too real. He strokes the straps of a sister's bag with his thumb.

"My choice," Bree adds, as if oncology has somehow become her chosen area of expertise and a subject she is most qualified to rule on.

As Eileen offers her view, ("Bree, I wouldn't be stubborn on something like this,") William heads into the guestroom with their bags. He will put them here at least temporarily, for his money's on Bree to win that argument. Nonetheless, he desperately hopes she concedes on these other fronts. Maybe the sisters can take the lead in convincing Bree to change her mind in ways he can't. For didn't his wife always say the Overton girls always came together when troubles joined? As children, their motto was 'one for all, all for one,' and they always did best when rallying round. If her siblings could persuade Bree to resume chemo, he certainly wouldn't mind being pushed to the sidelines here or at the hotel, whatever they need.

As he opens the guestroom closet to put away their luggage, he is surprised to find his golf bag stored there. He had forgotten about this bag he's used so infrequently over the years. That proud monogram and nameplate, WD, attached to the glossy leather now seems to mock, *Who's WD?*

Years ago, bored on those weekends when Bree was stuck chauffeuring the kids to and fro, Dr. William Durning had sought out new friendships through golf. Back then, nearly all his colleagues were avidly taking up this game of tepid putts and wild-assed swings. Most had graduated beyond Sunday sports in front of their T.V.s. to mornings where they'd stand and kick mounds of dirt, then drink themselves into snoozes that erased all memories of poor performances on the green.

Bree must've found this closet a convenient place to store the clubs once he'd admitted to disliking the game. A trip to California and a course near the ocean had done the trick. He'd wandered to a cliff's edge in pursuit of a confounding eighth hole and instead found himself looking down on water so green, whitecaps lopped like cabbage heads, an Irishman's stew. In that moment, he'd felt a terror rise within. For right then he knew his own hands lacked the power, the skill, to move this ball in any direction; instead, a scheming Monterey wind would carry it out to those mocking green-when-they-should-be-blue waters, those teary ocean waves just beyond a salt-stained flag. And what would it matter? How would he fail, swinging into a wind? It had taken the vaulting encouragement of a three-iron stroke, the ball moving

28

beyond any glimpse he could see or hear, and only the dank bite of sand-laced air coming up on his tongue to remind him: *life can be grasped beyond unsteady moves.*

Later, it did not matter when William reminded himself such fears were illogical, primeval even. He knew he no longer would play golf or enjoy outings with others. And he wasn't eager to sit on bleachers cheering on Corey or Sophie at their soccer games. Instead, he'd turned to running.

The running proved addictive. Every morning, he would massage his shoulders and ankles in wide clockwise rotations. He also took care to eat and drink in ways that cleaned out the toxins. Until he felt stretched as a rubber band physically, emotionally, and he could move out onto unfamiliar paths without a moment's pause. By syncing every thought with his steps, he even came up with a mantra to carry him forward when the fatigue kicked in, *hold on, hold on.*

Now hold on, hold on—it is a state of mind he should perhaps revisit. For the briefest moment, he considers a jog at dusk to relieve his stress. The ache he feels in his shoulders after bringing in the bags, though, says otherwise. He pulls the golf bag from the closet then sets it down, feels relief instantly in his knees, his shins.

But hold on. Remembering the many ways he has benefited from self-care in the past, he feels these thoughts can't be dismissed.

For it's also true William has forfeited endless opportunities to escape with friends on 'boys' nights out' or weekend trips. Instead, he gives his patients the extra time; night sessions twice a week, Sundays if asked. Sure, he bitches occasionally with colleagues about the tough cases, how they drain, but he is committed.

Beyond this, there's only Bree. And he might as well face it—now that her cancer has returned, he will be facing an unbearably lonely future. In the next few months or years, he is going to sail out on whitecaps as crushed and insignificant as any golf ball. Sure in his heart, he does feel sorry for himself, for the future he can see without her near. How bobbing and endless and polluted those waters, how dreadful it will be skimming them alone.

There's a soft knock and as Eileen opens the door, he reels in the self-pity. His sister-in-law enters the room. Against the chintz armchairs and low, curved furniture, she stands tall as a guard on any basketball team. It must be awkward for a woman to be so tall; William always felt sorry for her in that way. Nevertheless, Eileen is a capable girl who seems certain of her every move. In that sense, she strikes him as the toughest and most attractive of the Overton trio.

"William, you're in here?"

"You found me."

"Oh, you're looking tired. I'm not surprised," Eileen says, noticing his haul. "You don't have to bother with our luggage. We voted and we're staying at the hotel. Also, we're inviting you and Bree out to dinner."

William realizes she couldn't have guessed he'd been eavesdropping; he feigns surprise.

"A dinner out? That's what you want?"

"Um hmm." Eileen moves to a mirror hung on the wall, checks for a lipstick bleed.

"Maybe you two should just go with Bree, get some time alone with her first," he demurs. "I'll see you often enough in days to come."

Only then does she turn and surprise him with an accusation, "Bree says she's not going to pursue chemo. Is that right?"

William looks to the floor and notices one of his shoes is untied. His sister-in-law's being her usual blunt self, yet he can hardly be surprised. Still, Eileen needs to realize they're on the same side. By joining forces, they have their best chance to convince Bree to stick with her treatment. All for one and one for all.

As he kneels to tie, this is what William thinks. What he says upon rising is something else, "That's what she announced a few days ago, yeah."

Eileen's glance meets his.

"William, what am I missing here? You're not going to push her to continue?"

"Missing?" he manages. "My wife wants to leave treatment and I have to accept her wishes. That's called respect. You can't do the same?"

"Will, I don't understand. Help me out."

William, but he doesn't bother to correct her. Somehow Eileen seems to be missing the central tenet of any decades-old marriage—compromise is often not compromise at all, but the lie of a white handkerchief being raised to win time, rethink strategies. Gather the troops.

And already, he is losing a sense of how to best reply.

"What's not to understand? I'm trying to respect her wishes on her treatment. I'm giving her my patience, shutting up."

"But isn't this the same woman who was eager to step up for any clinical trial three years ago?"

"I'm well aware," he grumbles.

31

"So. What's changed?" she demands. Usually Eileen's pragmatic style can be admired, but William is simply feeling bulldozed today.

"She's very tired," he volunteers, and he hears himself sounding almost helpless sharing this obvious truth.

Eileen's eyebrows lift briefly.

"If we give her some fun, a second wind, then she'll come round?"

Here is his moment if he is only brave enough to signal his agreement, *Of course, I'd love your help convincing her.* Still he's resisting even this for some perverse reason. For all her credentials as eldest sister in the Overton trio, Eileen no longer knows the woman Bree has become—the wife who hates the way cancer forces her to lie in bed while visitors speak in hushed tones downstairs. To her sister's queries William can only affirm Bree's need for dignity in the face of unavoidable absences, parrot once again words that might explain away her long rests: she wants to feel strong, not weak, strong, not weak. Chemo always seems to turn her in the wrong direction.

He rubs his tongue against his gums where they feel sore. Bruxism. That's what the dentist had diagnosed, attributing his teeth grinding during sleep to stress and recommending, of all things, a mouth guard sized for a hockey goalie. "So I should wear a mouth guard, that'll be sexy, huh?" he'd joked with Bree, only to find himself irritated when her expression came back long and pitying.

"It's different this time," is all he can think to reply. "The doctor practically told us on our last visit, 'This is it.' They'll offer her chemo and meds to hold off on strictly palliative care for as long as possible. But when that slide begins, it's really a rational," He clears his throat on the next word, can't get it out.

"What? An irrational, you said?"

"No, the opposite. No."

His sister-in-law frowns. "It is. Irrational, as I see it."

"Like I said, I'm letting her lead."

"You're either lying to me or fooling yourself. But there's no way after everything you two have been through, that you can come to the last lap and pass on a few more good months."

"We're running on empty!" he snapped. "You can't buy that?"

Buy that, he said. As if Eileen has inadvertently stumbled on some truth hidden in this closet. No, Bree didn't want the extra months and he couldn't force her. His wife was acting so differently this time. Three years ago, they'd worked together to minimize any time lost due to an initial misdiagnosis from an imbecile GP. She'd looked to William to insist on a CA-125 test with a specialist: he had. And then he had been William Miles Durning, Bree's WMD, her secret hero, her champion.

So why wouldn't he find himself confused now? That she didn't want to do chemo again, blacken the calendar with appointments. Or have him wash her in soapy baths after her heaves at the toilet, bleach the sheets when she soiled them. Remember when her stomach was popping stitches and he'd joked that cleaning her reminded him of boiling Corey's diapers in their first old rental on Belham Street? The two chores seemed much the same.

For then he'd peer at the raw insides of his lover, confront this soil-black underneath, and summon forth a gardener's hands-on confidence for a seeding. Not a mystery that these black loam stitches peeked up out of pulped flesh. But here was his place to go, his invitation

33

to dig. Laying down gauze, then sponging down...All those gentle motions he'd made in the bath, in their bed, conjuring intimacies they'd never shared before. Sometimes, those touches brought both of them to tears. What more could he have done?

And what can he do now but use these same hands to dig for her again, bring up another season?

This time, though, Bree doesn't want that kind of attention. He'd thought such tasks had fulfilled them both, but no, she was telling him, no. It seems Bree now only wants to fight something he can't touch or see, and who is he to say she shouldn't? Better to be Sancho, willing to escort her in this fight. Accept any role as long as she will let him stay by her side.

"What she wants," he says in a voice he usually reserves for his patients, "is to conserve quality of life. To make those choices for as long as she can."

Maybe it is the pomposity of his words, but Eileen snorts, "Quality of life, yeah."

"It's what we expect everyone to understand by the way," he snaps. "Anyone who shows up, friends, you, the kids."He utters these words with such force Eileen falls silent.

Eileen bites at her lip and William senses she is ready to let go of their argument. She confirms this by no longer studying him, but the room.

"This plant," she announces and moves to a wilting fern near the window. She slides a dulling leaf between her thumb and forefinger then picks up the pot and walks out of the room. William can hear her opening cabinets in the bathroom across the hall.

When she returns, she is also holding a plastic pitcher filled to the rim. As she situates the plant back on the windowsill, some water accidentally splashes on the carpet.

"I brought extra for the others I noticed that need help in the den," she explains as she tips to pour.

~4~

As with most everything else involving these sisters, the restaurant off the hotel lobby has been chosen by Eileen. Bree knows of far trendier nightspots in the area, Long . Island is her turf after all. But no, she won't fight this; she'll go with the flow. She grabs at whatever conversation is being ping-ponged across the table by her sisters, tunes in to Eileen's pronouncement, "Bree gets to pick."

"We all get to pick," Bree defers. "Or we can order different dishes and share."

"Either way. As long as I'm not cooking," Eileen says.

Claire laughs and agrees. "You're not, thank god. You hated cooking for us every night when we were kids!"

"Well. Who wouldn't? Little Red Hen me."

A waiter approaches their table. His glance moves to settings and with a flick of his thumb, he straightens the spoon Claire has just employed as a baton. With the impish grin of a child caught having bad manners, Claire shrugs at her sisters, settles both hands in her lap until the stranger leaves. Only then does she lean forward. A lamp hanging above their table casts a greenish glow above her face. With those soft cheeks and lipstick-slash smile, she truly does remind Bree of one of those punching bag clowns, the kind weighted with sand at the bottom. The sisters are having their effect; finally, she is relaxing enough to make such connections. But she still needs help. When the waiter returns with the wine, she asks him to pour all around. She also notices Eileen shaking her head even as Claire mouths silently, 'It's okay, no chemo.'

"Claire, Eileen, it's so good to see you," she exclaims, raising her glass. "When I heard, oh, the cancer is back, I didn't want to see anyone. I was wrong. You're the only ones who understand."

Her older sister raises an eyebrow.

"I mean, you both know to relax around someone who's sick." Bree digs in the breadbasket for the last of the rolls and takes a bite, tastes onion. "After Mom's stuff."

"Mom's stuff," Claire echoes cheerily. "So this is a morbid reunion?"

"I don't see it that way," Bree says.

"No? Then how do you?"

"I don't know." And now it is her turn to shrug.

"We coped back then, yeah." Eileen fetches a breadstick from the basket and rolls it in her mouth, looks a bit absurd before biting down; tycoon with a Cuban.

"Sophie called," she volunteers.

While Bree's surprised by this news, Claire's the one who challenges their sister. "She called you?"

"She called her aunt to ask why their mom has been pushing them all away since this diagnosis? I promised to find out when I visited," Eileen explains. "So there. Now no one can accuse me of not laying out agendas beforehand."

Bree registers Eileen's defensiveness, the way she slaps the laminated cover of the menu hard against the table's edge in support of her niece and nephew. But Bree's aggravated too.

"It's not Sophie or Corey. Or William," she snaps. "It's me wanting some space."

37

"When the fatigue kicks in, right?" Claire prompts.

"Not even. I don't know. It's not like before. Half the time, I feel side effects from the drugs or chemo are going to do me in. And this diagnosis is terminal. So what's the point of letting the doctors have their way with me until it's too late?"

Bree smiles then realizes both sisters are nodding their heads as if to commiserate, yet seem thoroughly dismayed.

"I'm just looking for a break," she says, terrified even this truth will be scrutinized, and yes, Eileen's response signals she has those intentions.

"Turn off your phone when you need to, then," the oldest sister scoffs. "But let your family in."

"Oh sure. Turn it off and then all their voices are in my head. Mom, what do you need? How can we help? Hours out of chemo and I'm stuck figuring out to-do lists for everyone else? When did that become the way it's supposed to—? I mean, we, we learned how to disappear when Mom took a turn for the worse."

"We were kids, there's no comparison."

"We sensed what she needed," Bree insists, waving her fork in the air. "We didn't cause anyone trouble. Do you know I've never known other kids to be as quiet as we were?"

"Why would they be?" Claire starts to say, but Eileen interrupts.

"We were kids, that's the point. Sophie and Corey are adults who can actually help their parents. You should let them, Bree."

As Eileen's face seems to come at her, Bree blinks. The table no longer separates the three sisters in any safe way.

The waiter returns with their orders. Despite earlier confessions of diets, all have been given large portions. The Overton girls fall silent as they eat until Eileen once again raises the debate, "The thing is you're textbook. Everything you're feeling has to be tied to depression in some way. But why aren't you letting William help? It's what he does for a living, for God's sake!"

"Maybe he can't treat relatives? There's some ethical code he has to follow?" Claire chimes in. "I once asked for his help and he never—."

Eileen cuts her off. "Not now. This is important. Bree, I'm not saying he needs to be your shrink. But your aversion to the chemo—you should talk to a therapist on that one point before you decide. It just doesn't make sense. In this city you've got Sloan Kettering, one of the best. All the stuff they do these days. Chemo can buy you time and who can guess how that might go for you?"

"Ah, the chemo."

"That's right."

Bree straightens in her chair; the slats come up hard on her back. Clearly, she has forgotten the absolutism of the eldest Overton girl. When Bree had faced chemo the first time, Eileen researched reams of information on the Internet then shipped her the printouts. At her own job she fought for a compassionate family leave, secured three months, and came out to help. She'd tended.

So, what was Bree thinking? Eileen couldn't possibly accept her plan to cut off treatment this time. To give over, surrender, when she and William both stood ready to serve...

Still, she can't conceive of taking up the fight this time. Already in her mind, she is unlatching. Shifts in concentration helped her get through chemo years ago, but now this pleasant state of drift seems to elude her. She's been feeling quite lonely as a result, no matter who's near.

Perhaps she's looking a bit panicked for both sisters slyly trade glances. Then Claire offers, "Bree, come on back to my room. We'll relax before William picks you up later. Eileen you're welcome too, but not if you're going to go on about the chemo. Give it a rest, why don't you?"

Eileen sniffs, "So you're taking her side."

"Every time," Claire says smugly.

Two beds and a dresser are placed in angled corners of the room opposite a window's view. A pattern of black and yellow swirls in the carpet proves slightly nauseating, unsettling to Bree.

"You like? Stay," Claire invites as she unzips her bag. "Call William and tell him to bring over a bag for you."

"I'm tempted," Bree admits. She and Claire could hide away here much as they had years ago. They could be brave in each other's company. "But the room doesn't seem big enough. There's not even a pullout couch."

Hands on hips, her sister looks about and frowns. "Wait. This will help you decide. No pullout couch, but ta da! A mini fridge stuffed with all kinds of treats. What can I do to persuade? Wine?" Claire opens the door, peers in. "A California label, so not the worst."

"I can't. I've had too much already on these meds."

"I can't convince you? And here we've come all this way."

"Not fair. Be fair." Bree spies a coaster on the table. She picks it up and palms the small rounded weight. "Thanks for backing me up with Eileen though."

"About the chemo?" Claire makes a face. "Not even a question. You get to decide. You know Eileen, she gets things in her head. For my money, she's the most rigid, righteous—."

"Claire?"

"Yeah Breezy?"

"No nicknames, okay? Or turning on each other?"

"Sure."

Bree puts down the coaster and makes a small tour of the room. She moves as William might, adjusting a notepad so the Marriott logo can be read, fingering a drape cord.

"Everyone else wants me to be strong," she confesses. "I mean, they don't say that; they say the opposite, 'It's okay, you can lean on us.' But getting through treatment's still a solo act as far as I can tell."

"You sleeping okay?"

"They're giving me something for this, something for that. That's not what I want to talk to you about."

"Sure."

Even as Bree gathers her thoughts, she realizes she will be improvising again. This entire evening has seemed hedged with unexpected turns, detours she had hardly anticipated when she'd asked her sisters to visit. So, what does she want from either of them now that they've arrived to care for their dying sister? Not Claire's nervous quacks surely. But is her younger sister's nonsense still her best rejoinder to Eileen and William, and all their indisputable facts that threaten to overwhelm?

"Well. I mean—I don't want the confusion. Not at this point." Bree draws the words out slowly to boost her own resolve. "I just want to get past all this. I'm so tired."

"Okay."

Bree pauses at the window, fingers the burgundy drape's fold.

"That's miserable to confess. Don't share."

"I won't. But listen to me. You're brave, girl," Claire volunteers.

Brave. Not once in all this time has she felt brave. What's brave about frantically trying to cast off what's crawling up onto you like a flea, a mouse: get away!

"How I'm acting doesn't make sense, I know," she admits.

"It does to me!" Claire also lowers her voice as if ready to confess. "Something happened to me too, Bree. I don't usually share it but I'll tell you. Because you're being so damn brave and smart."

Her sister smiles and Bree can see where her lipstick has slid unnoticed onto skin.

"You'll probably think I'm the one who's crazy when I tell you. No, I mean it. I'm the one who needs to see William in therapy, not you."

Claire sits on the edge of the bed, her hands working the air. Bright garnet and onyx rings, gold-colored bracelets, swing in accompaniment to her words.

"First, I'm gonna say it wasn't the vodka I drank that night. Maybe I had two glasses, that's all. But Frank and I were on the couch in the den, the girls weren't home—no listen, I'm telling you for a reason. I mean, well, we were making love. Then in the middle of everything I felt like I was going to faint. Everything I could see in the room fell away and instead all that came up in front of me was all this grey. Like a fog crept in and I'm supposed to guess what it means."

"What does it mean?"

Claire kicks off her shoes and leans back on the bed. Her palms flatten against the spread.

"Along with this grey," she starts up again in a voice so low Bree has to abandon her spot near the window to hear. "I'm not going to say it was a voice exactly, but a real clear thought. Nothing exists, God's telling me. But carry on anyway."

"I don't—."

Claire interrupts, her words gaining speed. "*Nothing exists.* I'm not saying I've seen the light or I'm born again or anything, because I'm not. But this wasn't good news I was getting; this was the opposite. Nothing exists, God said. But carry on anyway? I heard all those words so clearly I got the chills, you know. Like there was something coming and I was more frightened of it than I've ever been in my life. I asked Frank the next day, 'Was there anything you saw?' No, he was getting his rocks off; we were having sex. That's all that happened as far as he was concerned. And for me afterwards? My life's just the same. I know this sounds so crazy. If your husband was listening to this, he'd lock me up, probably. But do you think I'm?"

"No."

"You're looking at me—."

"I'm not looking at you in any way. I don't know what to say, Claire."

Claire shrugs, a shamed assent.

"Well, don't worry, I don't need to hear. I just wanted to help you feel okay with your stuff, so I told you."

Claire's hands chop at the air as if she's trying to break up any strangeness in her words, make them small. Still hoping this all might be an elaborate joke, Bree studies her face a bit longer then finally suggests, "Nothing exists. Carry on anyway. But you had to be drunk."

Even for Claire, it's an odder narrative than usual. Her sister can claim seven moves over eleven years through towns in Binghamton, Albany, Rochester, Syracuse; Manhattan too. She has played house in ranches sporting faulty alarm systems and broken screen doors, been kicked out of rentals by landlords months before her leases came up for renewal. Bree always considered Claire's explanations for acting badly more embarrassing than her actual behavior.

But all her flights seemed to pivot around escapes from monstrous lovers. Worse, they affected her children when they were forced to change schools mid-year. When Bree last saw her nieces at a family gathering, the oldest girl was pierced in too many painful places to simply call it fashion; the youngest had gazed at a T.V. screen the entire time. Bree couldn't help comparing Claire to a child shaking out the last of her piggy bank, trying to scavenge up something from what spills out. But too often, her girls were all that clattered forth, the last investments their mother could lean on while facing her next botched romance or lost job.

Now she pushes aside her own chaotic thoughts to focus on her sister, *what's going on here?*

"Claire," she prompts as gently as she can. "All that fogginess? Maybe it was a warning to slow down if you feel you're losing your grip."

Claire listens quietly then surprises Bree by grinning her way.

"I think the message is you can relax, Bree," she says back. "We go, our kids go, our homes are already gone.

44

There's no legacy left behind. We fool ourselves hoping there might be. But carry on anyway.

"God said it to me that night, right? So I'm going to be religious even though usually I'm not. I'm going to believe and be born-again with all God's told me."

Making another small noise in her throat, Claire rolls over until she's lying on her stomach. With her sister's expression partially hidden, Bree starts to relax. No, she doesn't need to listen to these confessions with any special care. Not this time. As usual, Claire's bulldozed past anyone else's problems with her crisis of the moment.

She hates to think William was right when he warned her to watch out for this sister's dramatic displays, but Bree's so easily seduced by her. It's always been this way between them. The biggest danger of buying into Claire's pronouncements is that you start to believe life can, indeed, be as she says. Our lives are fated, yes, fated, and against that roll of the dice, we're all doomed. Once you start taking such statements seriously, there's no reason to believe you'll have control over anything ever again...

Lowering her glance, Bree sees a small liquor bottle ostensibly bought on the plane and now tucked in Claire's bag.

"God was saying, get thee to AA, girl."

As she clues into the source of Bree's distraction, Claire sniffs, "Okay, okay," with no apology or explanation.

And there, Bree do you see? The Overton girls aren't the same. We're not connected in the ways we were in the past, emotionally or by circumstance. Bree has to cope with cancer now and how grim this season might yet prove to be. Eileen chooses to hide her worry for both sisters in endless lectures. Meanwhile, Claire hasn't been able to

45

hold onto anyone for years and so has trouble seeing past her own pain. She no longer tries.

Bree supposes she faces the opposite dilemma. Too many allies surround her these days. They all care, but none of them can actually help her. And they demand time and energy she can no longer give without resenting their intrusions. Their concern exacts too heavy a price and when will she finally be able to shove away such weight? Who else might be willing to help her do so? Not one of them, as far as she can tell.

~5~

Grocery shopping's definitely the crap of life, and William has spent too many hours of his Sunday checking off this list of to-dos. Secretly, he thinks his time is too valuable for these mundane tasks, but maybe he's not hiding his disdain too well; hadn't the girl at the register rolled her eyes when he bitched at the price of pears?

As he approaches his car in the lot, he notices snow is beginning to settle on the windows. He opens the trunk to unload his groceries then swings the now empty cart into one of those steel cages fiercely. As if he is bowling for that strike and couldn't care less if its wheels turn and threaten other vehicles or people in its path.

He belts himself in, clicks the locks, drives the seven blocks home keenly aware that lit streetlights are guiding him through. At four-thirty p.m., dusk is already descending. A row of houses flank the left side of the block, their brick exteriors transformed into milky whiteness under floodlights. As snow falls there's no real darkening, though. There's only Nature throwing its wet blanket on his overscheduled list of chores.

William has had no time to enjoy the season's turn this year. Rather he dreads it all as an endless mocking, *time's always in control not you.* He turns on the wipers, click, click, and eases the car onto their driveway. The Lexus hums just a bit to accommodate.

Carrying bags into the house, he finds Bree sitting at the kitchen table. The day's paper lies unfolded by her side on the table, the comics section slashed through with a pencil. His wife seems more interested in the storm outside. Her face is turned to the window, her right leg neatly tucked under her left so she might prop herself up, find a better view.

For years, William has been entranced by Bree's habit of folding her legs in ways that distinguish her in any setting. He has caught her in such a posture on hardback chairs, stools, on sofas at elegant parties. The other wives may be seated with low-slung blouses falling in accordion folds that accentuate their cleavage, but otherwise they hardly distinguish themselves in any visual way. In contrast, Bree seems to rise from these huddles with transcendent grace, much as the winged maiden kneeling on a cliff in those old White Rock ads.

William throws his keys onto a table by the door, heaves his grocery bags on the counter as Bree turns in her chair and smiles. He comes over to kiss her most dearly freckled cheek.

"What's the word?"

"Cornea. Fifteen words to be average."

"So what do you have? Corn?"

"Core."

"Near."

"Care."

"Cane, cone."

"Orca. Is that a proper name or allowed?"

"Proper, I think. Carne? Like carnival barker or something?

I'll look it up."

Her dictionary is never far from her these days; it's a book she trusts because on these pages words are definite

48

and blunt. Words don't hide away insidiously here; even the word cancer can't hide. She flips to the Cs.

"How many so far?"

Bree frowns. "Eight. We're not even close to average."

She picks up her pencil and tries to pretend this game and not the storm has held her attention. With the eraser, she pokes at her chin and William can't help but be moved, charmed. All he wants to do is sweep her up, but patience. It will be worth waiting until they can get to average.

For average in their home is synonymous with normal now and a life he would settle for in a second. Only three years ago, a big part of getting to "normal" each day had also been tied up with the comics section of the paper, the crosswords, the Jumble, even the horoscope's cheery predictions. Playing all those word games focused their minds on semantics they could control, while the rest of their world went mute with fear on Bree's diagnosis. Buoyed by these tiny victories each morning, they sought nutritional aids for beating cancer on the Internet by mid-afternoon.

Then William had not acted the part of a doctor but someone else: the hands-on nurse in this arrangement, mastering small movements to please his wife. Offering up a fresh-laundered towel, a massage, a smoothie, a bath. Back then, tasks required love from all those different drawers. They'd both been so proud of their finely executed partnership and certainly when remission came, the mutual gratitude they had for each other's efforts had energized the marriage for a good long while.

This time though, Bree wasn't allowing any kind of collaboration. These labored alliances over word games were practically the only intimate moments his wife let him claim.

"We'll get there, we always do. Don't give up yet."

"I won't."

But she lays the paper down, yawns.

"I had a weird talk with Claire at the hotel the other night," she says. "I wanted to tell you about it."

At the counter, he begins to arrange his purchases. Dinner will be sandwiches salvaged up from a loaf of bread and any meat stored in the lower fridge bin.

"Something weird from Claire? Surprise, surprise."

"No, really."

"Sorry. Go ahead."

"She was trying to help me."

"Sure."

"I'm thinking that's why I wanted to see them both. I guess I got to feeling nostalgic remembering all the ways my sisters and I survived tough times by sticking together. Ancient history, I know. But in some ways not, right?"

"That's right, that makes sense," he says, trying to stem his own jealous bite at her urgent need for siblings.

"Anyway, Claire gave me a different perspective off something that happened to her months ago. I don't know if she had a breakdown or something even weirder, but she's convinced it was transformative."

"What's that?"

With some hesitation Bree says, "She told me…this story about being drunk one night with Frank and in the middle of their lovemaking, no listen. She's overcome by, uh, could you call it a vision? A drunk hallucination?"

He can't help it; he makes a face. Then he unwraps bagged bread and pulls out slices, takes a mustard jar from

50

the refrigerator, a bread knife from the drawers, to cover up his first reaction.

"Sounds like Claire's usual drama."

Bree sighs. "Probably. I should tell you she was drinking when she had this, um, moment. But then she's telling me, God came to her. She saw all this grey. And God says to her, nothing exists. Carry on anyway."

"Well," he manages.

"What do you think? Have any of your patients ever—?"

"Had visions? Stories where they're confiding to God? Yeah, and not just the psychotics."

"Should I be worried? Is this, I don't know, Claire being too depressed and maybe dangerous to herself or the kids?"

"Not necessarily. Knowing your sister, it's kind of on the mark. She has um, an overripe imagination, let's say. And you said she was drunk. Drunk can do it."

He plugs in the toaster, hits the lift knob, and pulls two more pieces of bread from the loaf. With inordinate concentration, he watches the coils redden with heat.

"You want salad?" he asks, glancing at a half-dozen tomatoes lined up in soldierly formation on the sill. He doesn't want to hear stories of Claire. Claire irritated. Once he had tried to offer her some professional advice, but any appreciation on her part quickly devolved into therapy sessions by phone until he had to cut her off. She had rewarded him at Thanksgiving with relentless teasing. "William is so stoic when he's playing therapist, you can't make him flinch. No matter what stories you're telling, you don't want to lie, you want to tell the truth, right? Not with William. All I found myself wanting to do was exaggerate, shock him, you know? It's like he was asking for it."

51

He'd stayed away since.

"You think she needs help?" Bree presses.

"Not my call. It's hers, if she's unhappy."

"She didn't seem unhappy."

The last slices of toast pop up. He pulls at the crusted edges and hoots like one of the Three Stooges, exaggerating how hot. When she laughs, he's thrilled. Thrilled to fake a burn, play clown, anything to distract. He fills their plates and after taking a seat at the table says, "Look. I don't care about your sister. She's not my wife. You—I want to talk about you."

"Me?" She groans. "What's there to talk about?"

"So much. Everything. We have to make decisions."

"About what? There's nothing to decide this time. What pills to take? What pain to bear? Whether or not to take on chemo again? I'm not thinking about that stuff anymore."

"All right."

He feels a flip in his chest, but the argument is done. Like a quarter: heads or tails. Flipped.

"We're in this together," he tries in a low voice.

"But we're not."

Bree rises from her chair to rinse her plate. Bubbling water fills the sink, foams bracelets around her wrists.

"Really, I don't want to keep discussing this until you—," she grumbles.

"Until what, Bree?"

She doesn't answer. Normally they would have left it like that with one of them going to the refrigerator for milk or fruit, slamming doors until somebody flinched. But this evening, it is different. Bree dries her hands on a dishtowel then folds it neatly. Her nightly rituals will not be messed with and see, William? I'm not an invalid yet.

"Will you unpack the rest of the groceries, or should I?" she asks.

"I'll do it," he replies, seeing his own opportunity to bang cabinets in protest. As she leaves the kitchen, he does just that; slams, slams. But also, what's wrong with you Bree? I'm going to lose you and so you're preparing me? That's a cheap trick he uses on patients. He forces a break when they start to commit themselves to the therapeutic relationship in unhealthy ways. The same provocations are not to be used against him, the doctor, now.

With a shudder, he flips off lights in the kitchen then heads for the den. He darkens this room too as he enters. It's become necessary somehow that all signs of their marriage disappear in every room. It is easier to ignore one of his running shoes abandoned in the mudroom then, or her reading glasses laid on a nightstand in the bedroom. In this darkness, even the flowers he'd brought home two days ago will lose their romantic powers and exist simply as spiky shadows in a vase.

From the doorway, he can see slanted shadows in the den play off the blinds and decorative brass pots surrounding the fireplace. William also likes this miserly light because his poor attempts to clean on Carla's days off can't easily be detected. Dust bunnies may live under the couch, creases stamp pillows, but he can always minimize such impressions in the darkness, relax.

He picks up the remote and flips through channels on the T.V. but nothing draws his interest, soothes. Why is she acting this way? If he attempts to read her behavior as a psychologist, the answer has to be she's feeling desperately alone. That's not hard to understand. The cancer's ended many of her casual friendships as her pain cruelly isolates. *But why does she blame me for her loneliness too, when she's my love?*

Watching images move silently across the screen, he remembers a time in their marriage decades before. When fighting with Bree in a London hotel room, he'd turned on the T.V. to a BBC news report if only to drown out their noise against the walls. She'd laughed, mocking, "Oh try to ignore me. But there's not much to choose from on British television, just so many channels. Instead keep your eyes on me and listen to what I'm saying. 'Cause you also chose me once, remember? You picked me. I'm the one you can't take your eyes off, or shouldn't. I'm the show you'll be watching for decades, so you might as well settle in."

~6~

Downstairs, Bree can hear Carla knock the vacuum against chairs in her weekly hunt for dust. Normally Bree tries to stay away when she's working. Her job is to sit in the kitchen beforehand with a notepad and red wax pencil, make a list of Carla's chores for the day. Any small talk has surprised them both, at lunch or during laundry sorts. This is how Carla prefers it and Bree has usually obliged. But today she is feeling so frightened, desperate to claim any rights she can.

"Carla!"

The vacuum bangs away, suffocating her words.

"Carla!" she shouts.

She hears appliances being turned off and her maid walking up the stairs. Carla comes into the room smelling vaguely of vinegar. As she enters, Bree picks one blue headscarf from many laid across the bed and asks, "Can you tell me how to put this on?"

"I'm sorry, what?"

"I'm running out of ideas," she says, wrapping the cloth around her wrist. "You know, I get so tired thinking about how to dress myself every day. How I'm going to be dealing with all these wigs and scarves soon."

Carla begins to understand. She fingers her own black frizzed hair, asks, "How can I help you?" Bree thinks her husband with his patients couldn't be more diplomatic or kind.

"You could talk me through? Eventually, I'll need to do this myself."

Carla nods, picks a purple scarf off the bed. It flutters up in a fanning motion. But she seems so hesitant Bree has to urge her on. She steps near so Carla might be able to reach around her and wrap.

"Show me," she pleads.

Carla does so, not explaining as much as displaying tricks with scarves through her moves. She centers the purple scarf atop Bree's head then grabs the bolt of cloth at its ends. Her arms catch the light as she loops two ends of the material; Bree feels a definite but not uncomfortable tightness as the scarf wraps round and fabric softly crunches in each ear.

Carla leans in until Bree can hear her breaths. She tucks a bit of fabric into other folds and Bree peeks; Carla's made her a turban. Her face runs long underneath the acorn-shaped top.

"That's one way," Carla offers. "You like?"

When Bree pauses in her response, she hastens to assure, "If not this one, you have many more here. These colors bring out your eyes."

"My eyes are hazel," Bree demurs.

"Hazel?"

"Yes." Umber like a nut at the core, green as avocado at the edges. Carla comes close and with her own heavily lidded stare, appraises. Then she holds up one of the longer red scarves Bree has tossed onto the bed.

"Here you go. You could wear this scarf like a shawl, not just on your head. Like this. So, you're looking at this bright red in front. Like a robin, the color, you see?"

She centers the scarf across Bree's chest. Then with a short twist to the back, she ties the material behind her, lets the bulk drape along Bree's left shoulder. The image of her maid, this squat dark woman in her Mexico City T-shirt and blue sweatpants, bobs in their shared reflection.

But Bree hardly notices Carla fussing over details; she's stuck on the scarf. Or at least the scarf's color and its suggestion, *you can be a red-breasted girl, Bree.*

Unexpectedly tears well up to surprise.

It's a memory Bree hasn't had in how many years? Yet once before, glimpses of brilliant punch-red had tumbled to ground.

And she and Eileen and who else, cousins, all of them wearing Pinocchio noses still wet with sticky leaf juice ran to get help, "Come, come, a baby robin's fell from its nest, but it's still alive! We can save it if you come now!"

Bree's heart moved even faster than her feet; she was desperate to find a bird's savior if only to stave off Skyla's vicious pronouncement, "He broke his neck, probably." Her cousin who didn't even run with the others but walked smoothly into the Overton's dining room where aunts, uncles, and parents were arguing politics. Bree's voice is the loudest of all, "Come!" With her Pinocchio nose clamped onto a sloping nose roof and that pert chimney stem leading the way, she catches her mother's eye: *"Please, I'm not lying."*

Somehow this did the trick where nothing else normally would. Her mother squashed her cigarette into the Durkee gravy pooling on her plate and rose from her chair. She slipped off her brown heels when she reached the front door so she might move faster. Bree remembered this dash because her mother rarely acted with such concern for a world found past screen doors and closed windows. Usually when the girls brought home a cat without a collar or tear-shaped tadpoles in jars, she would stand at the door with one hand raised like a traffic cop, "Take it away!"

That day, though, Bree's mother had joined others on the cracked sidewalk to save a felled robin. Like any suitor, Mary Overton had kneeled to see if a heartbeat could be heard, then announced, "Be careful. If we touch it, its mother won't let it back in the nest." Yet in her next move, she scooped the fallen refugee gently onto her palm to carry it home. For she must've decided this time she could play God with one so young; this one time, she'd risk it.

In the weeks afterward, the robin became their mother's project. Its constant feedings weren't pawned off on the girls like other chores. She kept the bird in a shoebox in the shed behind the house and didn't let others in, not even Bree's father. Wearing rubber yellow gloves she normally used to wash dishes, she fed the peaked-beaked creature concoctions of water and pet store vitamins out of an eyedropper. One day she returned to the house after a feeding, her cheeks flushed. She threw the dropper in the kitchen trash and announced, "That's that." When Bree and Eileen looked up in confusion, their mother surprised them by adding, "You can go see."

In the shed, the girls found only an abandoned box, one of its corners nudged up in the dirt. Its tissue-lined bed was stained with grey and reddish feathers as well as streaky brown drops that made their eyes water, but otherwise gave up no secrets. Had the bird flown away or died? Their mother never told.

That wasn't the end of it though. All the sisters swore their mother had thrown out the medicine dropper she'd used to feed the bird. Bree herself remembered seeing it in the trash bin in the kitchen. So it was a frightening surprise when that dropper, at least its twin, popped up once again in a bottle of brown liquid on a bathroom shelf. The bottle situated high but at the front edge of the shelf so Bree could reach it. That was important, for her mother would routinely send her to retrieve this particular bottle. The medicine seemed to work as a curative whenever Claire suffered with her nervous stomach—all the vomiting and wastebaskets that had to be emptied afterwards—or when Bree had her fevers and lay with the sweats.

"Sit up straight now," her mother would direct one sister as the other watched. Then she'd give a quick thrust with the dropper under the tongue: three drops, four. All these years later Bree couldn't remember the taste, but it had to have been awful. For she could recall Claire's expression of absolute disgust whenever the bottle appeared.

And isn't memory a mocking intruder? Long and short-term?

Off her last round of chemo prep, she now has this slicing scar on her abdomen as thick as a traveling bag and oh, isn't she sexy? How much can any red draped scarf pull glances away from these purpled wounds? Who is she fooling?

Of course, she knows William is always careful not to show his shock whenever she stands nude before him. The first time she'd had to undergo debulking surgery, he'd given back only a game face when her body revealed

59

its scars. When the cancer metastasized near her lungs, they'd sliced so inexpertly she took to wearing sleeveless tees to bed and so denied him his greatest pleasure when they made love, breasts that could be gazed on for hours.

And now this: follow these new cuts pointing in all directions to confuse, repulse. What can anyone do to hide away this too-damaged self? What can they do right now?

"You have a skill, Carla," she murmurs. "Women like me, we need to learn how to wear these scarves. You could make extra money teaching us."

Carla smiles, showing an uneven row of teeth. "Oh, I'm not looking for any more jobs but thank you, Ms. Durning."

"Please. Carla, it's Bree. You're in my closets, my bathrooms, I feel like you know me better than most people in this town."

Carla gives her another halting smile. But Bree knows when it comes to erasing boundaries between them, Carla won't. She doesn't have it in her nature to be less than formal with an employer. She is perfectly legal; they'd checked papers when she was hired. Still she moves about this house like a person filled with fear, a traumatized product of Mexico City's slums.

Actually, it's surprising that Carla's acting this comfortably with her today. Her maid's knee pushes up the bedspread as she leans over for two more scarves; one a heavier cotton material darted yellow at the edges, the other a translucent grey.

She rises from the bed and steps over to Bree, glances at her quickly to make sure she's not offending. Then using her bare, coppery arm as a hanger, she folds up the scarves into neat rectangles and wraps them across her own head. With lowered eyes, she starts to hum a slow, soulful rhythm.

"You know my daughter?" she says. "She is a cook, wonderful. But she got many, many tattoos on her body. I do not understand why she thinks she should add this and that color until her beautiful skin is something else, like a snake on top of a violin, on top of this word amore. 'That's Italian,' she tells me. And no tattoo stops on any line, so you look and say, 'What's that then? Oh my. What is that then?' A rose for Opay—that is her husband's name—on her left, on her?"

She motions across her own chest until Bree understands, translates, "Her breast?"

"Yes, yes, the breast. I am embarrassed to say. All the time I am asking her, 'What is this and then you have this put on you?' But she has so many pictures you cannot look at any one for too long. 'Why do you do this, Marguerite?' I say."

Bree cocks her head. And yes, Carla's not showing much discretion as she points to her own breasts under the t-shirt, but her words intrigue. She has a daughter obsessed with tattoos, all those colors seeping through skin like wet teabags.

"What does she say?"

Carla stops in her rocking. Her face goes long as she confesses, "She says back to me, 'Oh Mama, oh Mama. To me, life is a world so full, I can barely take it all in. I want to share what I'm thinking with everyone else, and with these tattoos, I can. Without even saying a word, I can share and share and share.'"

She shifts on one foot and her voice dips as well.

"But I say, 'I am your mother. I washed you. I bandaged you. I put you in perfect white dresses, rubbed you in towels. I put you in a bed with new sheets every night. I kept everything that touched you so clean, not any dirt.' 'Yes, you did Mama,' she says. 'You did a good job on me.' But she says this to me, and I don't understand. Maybe my English is not so good. Then she says it again in Spanish and still I have trouble."

Bree steps back from the mirror, her glance shifting to the floor. Carla's padded slippers, the ones she cleans in, have left white marks of scouring powder on the wood. She knows what Carla's saying, how a mother's love for her children doesn't always translate back even when they're grown.

But how can she expect Bree to respond? When her own mother had appeared in this very room only moments before, leaving her feeling like quite the child again; confused, full of questions.

"So, did you decide Marguerite was right?" she asks.

"I'm saying the tattoos. They make me think about her often."

"You worry for her."

"Yes, I worry. But that is all right," she sighs. "I am her mother. What else should a mother do?"

What else, what else? But pick the bird off the street even if touching it meant its own mother won't go near it again. *And you knew the danger, you warned your kids not to touch. Then you did what you wanted anyway.*

Why is she thinking of this again? Bree turns back to Carla, trying to regroup.

"Yes, sure."

"So much of the time she's telling me how the tattoos make her feel pretty," Carla says. "But to me they are the opposite. Like mud on my baby, she will have to explain when she is old. That's why I'm——." She breaks off, her words bolting to her own confusion.

"Don't stop. Please, go on."

Please, because Bree's own scars suddenly seem small and tame when she compares them to Marguerite's multicolored tattoos.

Carla shrugs and inches away from the mirror.

"She has decided that the pictures she puts on her skin now she will wear as a grandma and all will be fine," she says. "But already, I see an old lady embarrassed by such things. A violin on her arm; a snake! As if these things will make sense when she's as old as her Mama. I tell you it is so hard to look, thinking how sorry my Marguerite will be when she is old."

Surely she can sense Carla's grief. Still, Bree reaches to touch Carla's shoulder to prompt her, keep talking. She knows it is cruel, selfish, but please, please.

"Maybe," she says, "It will go another way. She will be proud of all these stories."

She finds herself hoping Carla will agree. For it could be Marguerite might just find out her old age cloaks in marvelous colors. Her daughter may live a long and wonderful life.

While all signs point to another truth for Bree. Her future is coming up fast, mapped on every curve of her failing body.

Nonetheless, maybe she can also be proud of these scars. They whisper of ways she has survived so far, if nothing else.

After all, no one knows whether the bird lived or died; no one ever told.

Bree places her hand on the crooked line running down her belly. In the mirror's reflection, she follows its path.

~7~

"She locked me in my room. It was gross. No food or water. I mean, she locked me in there for a day and a night."

"Locked you?"

"Yeah." He shrugs. "She got mad finding my stash under the bed."

William raises an eyebrow. "C'mon."

"Twenty-four hours, she told me. Just like they lock down the drunks. And she kept to it, school the next day. I mean, if she does that, isn't it against the law?"

William wasn't going to rise to the bait of siding with one story or the other; he was tired of this game with the mother-son duo.

"Your mom's not going to jeopardize your attendance at school. She knows what she's doing on that front."

But internally, he fights a surge of anger against her extreme measures. The mother employs an old school parenting style; he isn't a fan.

"She's whacked, Dr. Durning. I'm telling you."

"Tell you what. Let's bring her in on this."

"Fine."

However Cal smirks before uttering the word, perhaps revealing a desire to set William against his mother. This is an arrogance he sees in many of his adolescent clients. He also guesses this teen may see his doctor as some gullible, uninformed fool and right now, he doesn't care to fight the charge.

As he leaves the office to get the woman, he tries to ignore his own rolling stomach. Up and down the same hall escorting the same patients and the insides churn up like a dull knife—nudging at him, prompting, *only three more hours before he can get back to Bree, two.* His desire to leave sessions for bathroom breaks has become urgent and he believes such physical discomfort has to be emotionally charged as well, in no small part tied to his frustration when Bree sends him to the office each day. "Sitting home watching me sleep isn't going to help anyone, so don't," she insists.

Still. Ushering patients to his office and back, asking them if they wanted tea as he was brewing a pot; in the last few days, green tea has become his only way to detox, calm.

Sari is drumming her fingers on a closed magazine in her lap when he beckons her. They exchange glances briefly then she rises from the chair and he senses she is as unimpressed with him as he is with her; it's been that way between them since their first meeting. Most of all, she'd informed William in that session, Cal's father is dead. As if nothing else could be causing her son's problems. When William gave over the expected condolences, she'd accepted the sympathy then took up more than half of Cal's scheduled hour with a recitation of her own injured complaints. William knew many parents tried to squeeze some fast therapy for themselves off their child's insurance coverage. But unlike others, she'd left her son for forty minutes in the waiting room on that first appointment. By the time William had been able to get Cal back in, he'd started at great disadvantage with the boy and never quite recovered. Sari hasn't been invited back since.

Today though, William will ask her to join them. The mother takes the left side of the blue leather couch while Cal fingers its brass button seams at the other end. Both wait for William to take the lead but he hardly feels up to the task.

"Cal says you locked him in his room for twenty-four hours. Is that right? How long, Sari?"

"From Monday to Tuesday at five, five-thirty, after I got off my shift at work, yeah."

"You didn't let him out in all that time?"

"Oh he tried to get out. He kicked in the door so now it needs fixing."

"She didn't even let me go to the bathroom," Cal accuses.

"You didn't respond? When he needed to go to the bathroom?"

"I didn't come at first because I couldn't hear. But when I did, I came by to help, sure," she retorts.

Cal leans forward as if sensing an advantage. "She didn't let me out for meals. She told me to drink water from one of Pandora's spray bottles if I was thirsty."

Pandora. It takes a moment for William to register: the boy's chameleon.

"Not the stuff he's spraying," Sari protests. "I was talking about the water he gets from the fridge first, then pours into the mist bottle. That water's perfectly clean. He's just playing you with this."

Stubbornly, she avoids William's glance and instead eyes his diplomas hung on the wall.

"Cal, go outside for a moment," he says.

The boy seems surprised that his plan to pit one adult against another has been stymied. But he rises from the couch and leaves them.

Now that William has Sari alone, he isn't sure what he's prepared to say. He does understand he has to hide any anger he's feeling. But Sari reminds him far too much of what he'd lived through as a teenager with his own father—the same lockdowns and uninvited intrusions, the same dramatic contests of will.

Plus, he doesn't want to be here. The doctor knows he isn't focused; the doctor is perhaps cringing inside.

No don't think that way. Concentrate.

"Sari, on one hand, this is all your business and I don't blame you for punishing him. I'm going to support you on that. But, you gotta let a person go the bathroom, get a drink of water when he needs it."

"Sure, he comes in here crying. But how 'bout my comfort, when he's bringing drugs into my home?" she grumbles. "I'm not so happy with you either."

"Oh? Why?"

She squints. "You knew he was smoking pot, but you never told me."

"Sari, we've been over this. If Cal doesn't feel he can trust me, he won't open up. Look, there's no excuse for his behavior, but let's put it into perspective. From what he's told me, Cal's just experimenting. He's admitted to a few times and shows no interest in anything more."

"It's illegal! In his school, you're caught with pot, you're expelled!"

"With a small i, it's illegal. But of course, you're right to worry about anything he could be caught with in school. Listen, next time you'll call me before you do anything? Before either one of you goes too far?"

"It's zero tolerance at Dowling High. So no, I can't be as calm as you."

68

He flinches. Zero tolerance. No more chances. Yet given Bree's own needs, he finds the concept repellent whenever it is launched his way.

"Sari, you've got to be his mom. Not his jailer. You didn't give him access to a toilet and that's illegal too. In most states, that's called parental negligence."

She blinks nervously, understanding his threat. *I can turn you both in at any time.* Finally. He's happy to drum up some fear so maybe she'll pause before putting Cal in danger again.

Nonetheless, his nausea continues on a heavy roll inside. Goddamn Superman this job. Changing capes in the last phone booths out there, all those dark, smelly places starved for light and air.

Patient Notes: Cal Stepen (11/17)

Last week, this adolescent revealed he has known "since it happened" that his mother has been lying to him about his father's death. The mother had initially informed Cal that his father died after driving into a tree, leaving out news of his intoxicated state at the time. Patient, however, is highly intelligent and old enough to put clues together off a community newspaper. He told me he went to the local library and read through published police reports until he found news of a local car crash fatality on the day of his father's death. The autopsy revealed the driver had been heavily intoxicated. He simply followed up with an Internet search to confirm.

Some points worth noting have played out in our latest sessions. The boy revealed this information, expecting me to be surprised. Such confidences offer up some evidence he might see benefits in our sessions together, which is gratifying after two months of therapeutic work. Indeed, trust between mother and son continues to be so minimal that our alliance may model the patient's only healthy relationship with an authority figure at present. He has not spoken of friendships with teachers, counselors at school, employers, or clergy, to date.

Questions to indirectly explore with patient in future sessions: did his father act in ways that encouraged communications between mother and son? Or did the father put pressure on their already tenuous relationship, given his own alcoholism and presumed stresses in the marriage? What role did the father play in the family's stability and/or dysfunction when he was alive? And how will the two survivors fill the holes left by his absence; will they find or lose each other tending those holes?

Nearly finished with his session notes, William puts aside his pad, rubs his eyes. He is unwilling to let these final thoughts fly away just yet, but why?

Why? He's a crappy therapist, he can't tune into anything these days. From all appearances, the boy's outlook is far more precarious than William's. He's a boy who lost his father without warning; William has had ample time to process the latest news about Bree.

Still, both of them have had the same punctuation to come up against: death. Sometimes William fears he can no longer help his patients with any objectivity. He is trained to employ any and all techniques to help them but now he isn't giving over shit. Instead, he puts out a sign like any charlatan and moves through a checklist of symptoms to help them heal. He has the steps of grief memorized and becomes impatient when a patient gets stuck moving through—denial, anger, bargaining with God, depression, and finally, acceptance. But how patronizing and insincere. Now facing Bree's illness with no hope of another remission, he only feels the fraud demanding his patients fall in line with some generic list.

With patients like Cal, he senses his incompetence at every turn.

It is Cal, a child, who can tell him about death here. What he has learned.

William will do anything to hear what he has to say.

The truth is he can barely stand sessions with patients these days. He has scheduled them out for weeks between appointments, beyond what they can bear. And now, he is the one looking to a teenager to guide him. Cal Stepen, guide me. You've had worse luck in your life than I ever will. I still have time to say goodbye to a loved one. You never did.

But tell me, please.

In my old age, tell me how I can be as strong as you.

I am so jealous to know.

~8~

The doorbell rings, barely giving Bree time to swallow her pills.

Their synthetic taste flat on her tongue, she heads downstairs and opens the door to a woman holding a foil-wrapped tin. She is wearing a red parka but no hat or boots, despite the snow.

"Bree Durning? Remember me? I'm your neighbor Rebecca Glenn, five houses down? I just wanted to, well, drop off a meal for your family."

Her voice startles Bree. It sounds like a young boy's clang once puberty hits. All she can think to say back is, "Pasta, thanks so much. But how did you—?"

"You know, that's what neighbors do. We check in on each other. We do what we can when times are bad. And you're on the neighborhood list."

"Right. The list." She has a vague memory of neighbors at the far end of their subdivision routinely trying to organize block parties, check on rumors of illness and unkempt lawns. When Corey needed to augment his college applications with charity work, she'd pushed him to find out if they wanted volunteers. But she hadn't thought of these good-hearted scouts since.

"It's funny how we've lived so close by all these years, yet we've hardly talked."

Bree can barely make out her features under that furred hood but she senses this gentle tone is reserved for

72

people suffering with conditions the woman greatly fears yet can't ignore if only for one nagging thought, *Thank God, it's not me.* She tries to smile up gratitude anyway.

"I'm sorry. I don't recall seeing you and your husband on the street before."

"Oh we got divorced, you didn't know?" the woman explains cheerfully. "You've probably seen me walking my shelties, though. I have two now, a brother and sister. So someone walking her dogs in all sorts of weather? That's an empty nester or someone coming off a divorce guaranteed."

Bree takes a step back. She is getting so tired of people pretending every tough scenario has its upsides if one just looks hard enough. She manages to lean up against the door, signal her goodbyes. "Well, this is so nice. Thank you."

The woman's smile goes soft around the lips. "I'm happy to. Anything else I can do? Just knock on my door."

"Thank you," she says again but closes the door before getting an address. All her energy has to be summoned up to not say anything that might have been viewed as stupid or ungrateful, but she feels humiliated. All her personal business is out on the street now. Maybe she'd been naïve to think that she could keep her troubles private, but she had.

She heads into the kitchen and without even pulling up the foil to assess, throws Rebecca Glenn's good intentions in the trash. Yes, people bringing over food always mean well. But these days, she is not feeling grateful. Really, I don't know your life and you don't know mine. We talk to each other across hedges, at mailboxes; we don't know the skeletons rattling about.

73

She gets a glimpse of her face in the toaster's metallic reflection; how hard and angry she appears. It's true Bree's done the same in past years, sent food and magazines off to a sick neighbor as death and baking are tied into the routines of every neighborhood, all generations, and who can escape? For if we make these tributes, maybe some other person on our block will be sacrificed to angry gods on the mountains; we might yet be spared.

She makes even more of a monster's face at the toaster before busying herself with dirty plates in the sink. The truth? She feels like a failure accepting meals offered up to lighten her load. This used to be *her* kitchen, *her* point of pride. Now everyone, even William, assumes she can't keep up with cooking for two. When she was a child, their kitchen had been intruded upon in the same way after her mother's accident. Food was shoved at the Overtons all the time.

The memories come up, nauseating as boiled milk...

Everyone paid too much attention to her mother's limitations back then. All those strangers hovering about, scavenging in their refrigerators, cabinets, closets, for whatever was needed by the patient in the moment. The family's lives open to everyone's inspection at all times. That attention had been so draining, yet addicting too. Yes, addicting.

Eileen wouldn't touch any platters the neighbors left for them. She regarded each dish as a fearful temptation and preferred to starve a twelve-year-old body already thin and long as a waxed bean. To distract herself from pangs of hunger when they came, she took on kitchen chores that others were trying their best to avoid. She'd stack dishes with such ferocity no one would have been able to tell

74

when the occasional forkful was scooped off a plate and into her mouth before rinsing.

Bree and Claire, in contrast, ate all they craved. They gorged on lasagnas laid in square glass containers; tuna casseroles that cried tears along Saran Wrap covers just like the saints in mourning ("Only condensation," Eileen said with a sneer). They had unending gifts of homemade apple pie, the sugary goo bubbling up from steamy crusts; deviled eggs lined up like bowling pins with cracked tops; something Mrs. Mendes called her chicken paprika surprise; also Miss Gladys' ("Call me Gladys like the gladiolas,") sour tartar sauce for fish, too much lemon but no one ever told.

After years such as those, believe in kitchens. Kitchens were places where people got better, where getting healthy depended on Wonder Bread and milk and mashed potatoes on the side.

While in bedrooms, visitors would only find fatigue and anguished sighs.

Rattled by such memories, Bree moves to the window. She peeks out to see neither Rebecca Glenn nor anyone else is about, then snaps the blinds shut. Only in private, can she find the breaths to calm herself. For neighbors can be kind or unrelentingly cruel on many fronts.

Remember each year when their Christmas tree stood in the living room, its steady decline clearly visible through the bay windows as December moved into May? As the season started up each year, the Overton girls would be enthralled. They adored draping the tree with homemade ornaments, so never mind glittering whatzits and tinseled tie-ups; a trunk load's worth of cardboard rocking horses, scotch-taped angels, glossy dinner entrees torn from magazines and pasted on oak tag. Prayers to Mother Mary and Baby Jesus were strung up too so Mom would heal quickly after her car accident; these crayoned missives only able to hang cockeyed along the needled branches and no candles allowed. Instead flashlights were sometimes snaked up along the tree's trunk, clicked on.

"Trees don't come down until January sixth, Three King's Day," their father insisted each year. Decades later, Bree learned from a priest her father had been absolutely correct in his understanding. Nonetheless, January 6th somehow always gave way to January 7th and then all the months more. The tree dried and crackled, turned satchel brown at its fingered tips. Still everyone politely ignored its palpable decay. They closed the pocket doors leading to the living room and walked the house silently, as if a second invalid had joined their mother. The tree would stand for months until their father came home from work one day yelling, 'Too much to do and who goddamn cares?" Then he'd take a Stanley wrench to its bolted stand on the living room floor.

Until that day each year, Bree would ride home on the school bus only to see Christmas lights looped around the roof's gutters. As the bus turned the curve she'd think some kind of April Fool's joke was being played on her. For by then, they were in that season and she could see the house as her classmates did from those school bus windows, could guess at the cruel remarks that would follow.

She not only suffered for her family's failures on tortured bus rides, but in school as well. In fourth grade, she was urged to bring in presents for a grab bag exchange with other students. Short of money and lacking the courage to ask her parents for help, she'd come up with the brilliant solution of wrapping her favorite novel, Marguerite Henry's *Brighty of the Grand Canyon*, in pickle-green tissue paper. She'd made a selfless sacrifice of passing on her most beloved possession as a grab bag gift. The deception hadn't fooled. When Aimee Saunders held up the well-loved book for everyone to see, Miss Reid frowned and took her into the hall. "That book isn't new, Brielle Overton, now don't lie. Its binding is broken and are you going to tell me otherwise? Are you trying to pass off something old and get something new in return? That's stealing."

Her face stinging with shame, Bree was quick to agree. Sure, she was a thief; add it to the list. A kid whose mother hadn't left her bed years ago had to have lots wrong with her and everyone knew. How many of her friends didn't guess she'd rinsed her sweaters with dish soap every night because she didn't have permission to use the laundry machine and was trying hard not to smell in class? Or that she'd learned the trick of combing out her hair with baby powder because sometimes after chores she was too tired to bathe. It didn't matter. She was the kid who lived in that Christmas-all-year house at the end of the block and her contagion wore through in all ways. No one voluntarily came near.

Coming back to herself now, she tries to lasso a bucking heart. Take a breath; take two more. And realize the dishwasher will get plenty of use today, maybe three loads or four. There will be a sparkling haul with every dish and glass receiving her attention; this kitchen will gleam.

But who is even interested in Bree's obsession with cleanliness now? When all those filth-stained narratives she'd known as a child are circling her again. These same fraught associations tied to food, smells, hard-faced neighbors stopping by.

"Isn't it enough I have cancer?" she moans to no one, to God Himself. "Why are you torturing me with these bad memories too?"

Maybe it hardly matters. Bree hasn't thought of her life as deprived in any way since her marriage. She knows well that she has a devoted husband, children and grandchildren who will never suffer neglect. However, none of these realities seem to calm whenever well wishers come by to remind Bree she's once again on their radar. For this is the house on the street where sickness dwells and she isn't able to escape any of it. Not cancer or these memories. Both attack mercilessly, at all times.

They exhaust her. She is exhausted. Today, she feels like one of those out-of-focus shots coming up on the T.V. when someone is missing for forty-eight hours and just a shoe or abandoned scarf is found in a ditch. Weight, height, coloring, all are accounted for. Still if she's somehow discovered, no one will be able to connect this person definitively to any photo or loved one's appeal; no one will be able to make a positive I.D.

~9~

She sits at the dining room table, her glass filled with juice threatening to leave a ring on the mahogany wood. She is writing something, a list, and then she is coming over to shove him gently up from his half-doze on the couch.

She stands before him in jeans and a man's shirt too long and boxy at the cuffs, his. When William sees what she's written, he feels all sorts of gratitude for her choice.

"I have a confession to make," she says. "I will spend millions of dollars, all our retirement savings plus any insurance money coming your way, on presents for our grandkids. With your signature on this contract I've drawn up we'll start right away. Also, I'll expect the spoiling to continue for every Christmas to come. You'll make up a batch of cards saying, 'Love Grandma' and they should help you keep up the charade for at least a decade."

"Okay."

"I am telling you their closets will be stuffed with presents from me. Toys will be stored for too many years because everyone will be feeling too guilty to throw them out. This game was from Grandma, this Lego set. And I won't be around to care that Goodwill isn't getting its due."

He grins. "Special items from the jewelry chest for the older ones?"

"Oh everything, even my engagement ring. Just not my wedding ring."

"All right."

Her smile fades.

"After my mother's accident, we were told just the opposite. We weren't allowed to ask for presents bought in stores. She was going to get better so she was all we were supposed to want or need. Then again, I don't have such a positive prognosis. So maybe I shouldn't really compare."

She tosses her list onto a table and her mood seemingly shifts.

"My eyes are tired," she complains. "Maybe I need glasses."

William takes it all in but counts on silence and his professional training to find out what's troubling her. His instincts prove sound as she says, "I can hardly explain to anyone what's going on. Maybe you. Maybe...it's just— it's as if the cancer isn't the worst thing. There's something else, but I can't figure out what it is. That sounds crazy, right?"

"It's frightening you?"

"It's only these memories I'm having. They're not good ones tied to us, or the kids. For some reason, I'm thinking about my parents after my mother's accident a lot, their divorce."

With a groan she pleas, "You're the professional. You must know what's going on. So can you give me a clue?"

William certainly has heard those stories. But he finds himself surprisingly unmoved by Bree's request. He hears himself responding with the cool, neutral tones of a trained professional.

"You're angry," he says, making the question a statement.

Bree walks behind the couch where he sits. The move seems deliberate; as if her need to stand where he can't see her is the only way she can speak freely.

"Oh yes, I'm angry. People come to you and you have skills. So what do you say when they confide in you? Can't you help me the way you help them?"

"You want me to help you as a therapist?"

Bree inhales softly then walks around the couch to face him.

"Am I asking that? Yeah, I guess. All these people want you to counsel them and you don't hesitate. But now I'm sick, right? So maybe I need your attention most—in that way. " She lifts a hand as if to continue then falters. "I'm sorry. But haven't you noticed how depressed I've been?"

Her glance meets his and William's not sure what his expression conveys. Of all possible changes he is willing to make for her, Bree wants this? A husband denying his unique role so his wife might instead have a therapist on call?

 Sure, she probably thinks he can offer up either posture on request. But people who aren't trained in his profession can't understand his need to create boundaries; how he routinely puts up his guard with patients even as he tries to help them. He will empathize, evaluate, but never go so far as to emotionally connect. For William has created an identity he carries comfortably into his office every day. The distance he's established between doctor and patient has always meant safety. He has made a life for himself where he doesn't feel he is a burden to anyone and no one is a burden in kind.

Now his wife is asking him to tear down those walls, give over his best! But he can have no clarity when it comes to Bree. No objectivity. No safe space.

81

"Don't, don't apologize," he says as softly as he can. "It's only—we've been over this before. If you need to talk, we should call someone else. Maybe we can find a psychiatrist who deals with cancer patients and knows which antidepressants work best alongside your other meds. I can't prescribe so you'd have to find someone else for that anyway."

He can see her mouth go small, resisting.

"Maybe you'd do well with a D.O.," he offers.

"A D.O.?"

"A doctor who's skilled in alternative treatments. The guy you saw before, Trone? He was too much of a generalist. I'll admit you didn't click and I didn't notice early enough." His voice breaks, a mix of caution and nerves. "If I failed you before, Bree, I'm so sorry."

"No, of course, you didn't," she breathes.

"But anyway, it shouldn't be me. We still can," he says then stops himself. He's beyond scared to admit this truth. But given his best chance to help, William's sure he's coming up short.

His glance rivets onto that place she has always commanded in his life, the point of departure from all logic. Her hips. Once he had owned those hips. They had been his to undress, to come up against in a swirl of unthinking pleasure yet purpose, up down up down up down. When the feet are no longer needed to ground, but only the hips only the hips.

God, he wants to swing her into some other mood off these long, sick days.

He rises from the couch.

"No, not this," she says, but then lets him near.

So all right. He can be her husband and let that be enough.

82

He lowers his hand to her crotch, where she is warm if bone-dry. Her eyes close and she hums so quietly, he has to lean in. Yes, she will let him change the subject even if he can hardly forgive himself for the same. He needs absolution for not being able to protect her as a doctor might, from old or new pains. But when he approaches her unable to give her *that*, so *this* instead, she seems to understand that he doesn't deserve to be so tortured by such doubts; neither does she.

They head to the bedroom, his arm caging her waist. He can smell a scent on her, lavender beyond the medicine, wafting upwards like a genie from a bottle with a shape and texture and promise of wishes to be granted if only he is kind.

~10~

And so, Bree allows William to seduce her for the first time in weeks. She allows this as long as he didn't speak. Good now, don't speak. For she is so tired of talking and he must respect her silence too. He needs to realize she can no longer give her full attention to anyone—only this other force pressing up on her, grabbing from inside. This other, who does not come to her confused, repentant, but with unblinking intent; this force that digs deep to leave behind holes that will not be filled, never be filled, but merely abandoned as traps for anyone who might come along and stumble into all these hollowed-out cavities.

William groans mildly. His lips slide up and along her nostrils with a desperate need for her reassurances. She rolls her tongue into his mouth where the teeth are even and pearly-white fine. She tastes skin that has the smell of clean and can be licked lightly to bring up salt one day, the stubble of day-old beard the next.

With each embrace, she'll permit him to love, dig out what's evil, go on primitive alert. He can go down into wet, dark swamp, this fog and stink, to hunt. He can mine; scavenge. Sometimes he may even scratch and cause her pain in the digging, pain that she won't admit to because she loves him.

In turn, she'll give herself over freely—she'll submit to his grasping and stabbing and not resist. Even as his lips come up firm on her breast asking for forgiveness and her hand sweeps to his head as softly as any parent comforting a child, *I do forgive, I do forgive.*

If only because life now reveals itself as confusions she cannot think her way out of so she might move on, get at the air she needs instead.

Dear William,

I really can't explain, but I must get away for a while. Take a vacation, I guess. Not from you—my need to leave is not directed at you or anybody. I just need to go. And no, I don't know where I'm heading so I can't tell you. I don't know how long I'll be gone. But right now, I'm handling any physical pain and I have my prescriptions. So don't worry too much. I will call as soon as I have worked out a plan. Please trust me with this.

And yes, always love,

Bree

Part Two

~ 11 ~

What is she doing here, she isn't quite sure. And why Charleston, except her grandmother had always laid out stories of her childhood in some South Carolina town as if they were her finest tablecloths. She used to infuriate Bree with her refusal to admit the ocean coming up on Point Lookout's beach and South Carolina's coast were, in fact, one and the same, "The Atlantic, Grandma!" "No," her grandmother would insist, telling Bree and her cousins that jellyfish would circle a swimmer's thighs like hungry cats in Carolina's warm waters. While on Long Island's beaches, those same creatures could only slide helplessly by before swirling pockets of surf dashed them to the shore.

Of course, Bree's not looking to visit any beach on this trip, only check in to a clean hotel room downtown. With this choice, she has found for herself a view of white, pink, and yellow-painted homes trimmed by black iron balustrades across the street. Bree had imagined she'd feel energized by all this bright sunlight and pastel shading. What she feels most, instead, is the humidity. The wetness layers onto her skin not only in the usual places of pits, neck, knees, but even where her fingers meet her palms. She can touch skin behind her ear then hold a finger to her nostrils and smell a vaguely familiar odor of bologna and cheese sandwiches sitting in lunch bags for too long, staining their paper bottoms.

The wetness. For some reason, Bree hasn't anticipated feeling like a washed fruit with only one layer of skin protecting her from a pulpy underneath. The only part of her not wet in Charleston, she realizes, is down below. The part William would claim if he were here.

Maybe, though, this is just what she needs. A chance to expunge toxins through her pores when she feels unable to help herself in any other way. And while yes, it's hard breathing when the air drips with damp she doesn't have to confess that worry to anyone. At the very least, she is alone.

Bree unpacks slowly, wondering at the very fact of it—she is alone. She has done so much to insure this by heading to a city where she's never been before. Solitude beckoned the moment she fixed her glance to a poster above the travel agent's desk back home, urging her to *Visit Charleston!* She'd remembered Grandma Sue, her stories of growing up here, and suddenly desired nothing more than a flight without William holding her bags or heading into their hotel bathroom to make sure the tub showed no rust spots.

She isn't being fair, of course. There is no one Bree knows who asks less of others and forgives more. She loves William; she blames him for nothing.

But today, did he blame her? For her sin of flight, offering no warning? For a rambling letter he would no doubt discover on the bedroom dresser; will he take it as a mocking?

Don't second guess yourself, Bree. No, she isn't going to sit around regretting this trip when she simply wants a breather for herself. She needs to find her breaths where she can these days. And maybe this suite is much too large for one, but it promises her the space she needs. Besides she doesn't yet know how long she'll be here. Two rooms split by a half wall, a full kitchenette, a spa-sized tub in the bathroom, a stocked mini bar (even if it's not to be used to excess while she's on her meds; Dr. Sands' conditions were not to be questioned in return for the help he'd provided for her safe travels).

After her luggage is unpacked, Bree decides to hold off on a bath. Her blouses, pants, already hang in the closet and later she'll line up her shoes. But this is a walking city. Mostly, Bree just wants to open her door, pocket a keycard, go.

If she's feeling uncomfortable that she has for too long neglected this place where Jesus lives—well, now is the time to declare her allegiance.

When Bree was five, then six, and their mother confined to her bed, their father would take the older girls to church not only every Sunday, but yes Thursdays too. There, she was told to pray, pray in earnest for her mother's recovery. Both she and Eileen were taught to fall to their knees and shut their eyes so that their voices might rise in prayer without any distractions. Even decades later she still can remember the words of the prayer she'd been diligently tutored on, the one their father had cobbled together out of a few prayers so that any of Mary Overton's daughters could petition for their mother's recovery, memorize the words as soon as they could read. "Hail Mary full of Grace, the Lord is with thee. I come before you in the knowledge that you will help me. My faith tells me so. And my heart makes sure of this."

As children, the Overton girls were expected to blanket themselves in God's enveloping, all-knowing embrace, rather than parse out any moment or word for clear understanding. So when they had any questions, specifics were rationalized away. Bree only knew she had two Mothers called Mary, the mother of Jesus and her own. And it was fine if she also confused smells of burning incense with her father's Mennen cologne as he leaned down and told her to hurry, but not forget one word before she left the pew. For if prayers were stumbled through or forgotten, it could be a disaster, a sin, he'd warn. To drive the point home, he'd kneel to tie his shoes alongside Bree then snap his right suspender so the noise startled, "A venial sin. That's laziness. So don't forget your prayers." Then a snap to the left, white metal clips on his suspenders catching the light, "But a mortal sin comes with being defiant, not learning the words in the first place because you don't care. Is that what you want God to think about you, Breezy? That you don't care what happens to your mother?"

She vaguely remembers feeling damp, the beginnings of pee, when her father asked these questions. Still it is hard to trust such thoughts years on, sense what parts must lie forgotten or rise.

Standing in this church now, Bree suddenly feels dizzy, overwhelmed. She thinks she should sit, but leans up against a wall instead.

Then everything seems to move within: the truth.

She is Dennis Overton's daughter coming to the end of her days. She was once bound to a man who demanded she pray, pray, so her mother would never be punished for a child's forgetfulness (the suspender snaps). And may no

93

human being ever cause loved ones such pain as to forget urgent prayers that must be delivered on their behalf, or desert them in their time of need.

Until he did: their father. He left them all to be with the lady next door.

And now she has run from William and her children, those grandchildren she adores.

She has delivered this same cruel verdict to the people she loves most. But why?

~12~

"No one's angry," Corey says and right away, she knows he's lying. She can picture her son sitting at his desk in an office she's only seen once, when he gave her the tour. He'd escorted her past rows of burgundy partitions designed to break up the loft into cubicles until she read a nameplate on one: Corey Durning, Sales Associate. She noticed he'd tacked up a picture of Jessie but not the kids, over his desk. "I'm waiting for photo day at their school," he'd explained. Bree remembers thinking the place was too depressing for anything more than a starter job and Corey was five years in.

"We're not, but we did wonder why you didn't take Dad with you. Or at least, let him know you were going?"

His voice trails off and Bree feels for her son. He is treading so carefully around her emotional triggers, all these landmines. Another pause, then, "Are you scared so you took a breather? Is that it?"

Maybe, she considers. That would make sense to her son, being scared. Hadn't he done the same in his teen years, "run away" twice, worried them silly, even his father the psychologist who was familiar enough with adolescent rage. They shouldn't have fretted. Each time, he'd merely hitched a ride down to the cramped duplexes on Shore Road where some pimply friend, Greg or Daniel, had convinced inattentive parents to let their friend stay for the night.

"No, I'm not scared at all. I'm feeling energized by this city and I just want some time."

Bree stops, realizing how pitiful the word "time" sounds whenever she references herself.

"You're not taking the chemo down there, are you?"

She closes her eyes against his clumsy language, "taking the chemo"; her son is still so obviously uncomfortable with realities she's had to live with for years.

"No."

"So, I mean. Are you feeling strong enough down there by yourself? Why don't you let me call Dad and he'll——."

"Corey, that's my decision. Don't badger."

"All right." But her son sounds cautious, not liking this. She senses he'd like to ask if her departure might be tied to any trouble in his parent's marriage if only to hear her denials and be reassured. Truthfully, Bree's glad he's held back. She doesn't have such news to share, but also she can't forget how she'd planned this solo trip with such eagerness, excitement. Even now she doesn't feel a twinge of guilt when she thinks of the moment she chose not to include William, how quickly she'd gone there and no regrets.

Her oldest child needs something, though. His tone is pancaked in hurt.

"You're right, Corey," she confesses. "I didn't tell anyone my plans. To be fair, I didn't know them myself."

She hears her words and wonders: will he trust her? With Corey it could go either way. After all, he is their spoiled firstborn, a prince. They had great difficulty having him as she'd suffered two miscarriages before he arrived. But then she did get pregnant a third time and after fifteen weeks, sixteen, they were cautiously sharing their news once more, believing in possibilities.

"Do you want me to come down? I can make some changes in my schedule," he is saying.

"Corey, I don't need you or your sister. Or your father either. I'm perfectly at ease here."

"Okay." He tries to pass over a laugh. In his book at least, her crime of desertion will not be considered a felony. She knows he won't be as hard on her as the others.

"Corey, listen. At this point, I'm still in good shape. I don't need anyone to clean up my vomit or change bedpans." She grits her teeth. "And even if all that's probably coming, let me just have this one last vacation until then, okay?"

"Hold on for a second, can you, Mom?" she hears before his words garble. Someone must have approached him at work, she uses the silence to calm herself until he comes back on the line.

"Okay, I'm here," he says. "Have you called Sophie, Mom? Because if not, I can."

Sophie. Bree glances up into an unrelenting sun as she walks along. She stops, rifles in her purse for glasses that might cut the glare.

"I called your sister. We talked for awhile."

"Good. Everything okay with you two?"

"Why do you ask?" Bree says, trying to show only casual interest in his question. For Corey might have spoken with his sister and knows she is furious with her mother for this latest stunt. He might be waiting on her confession of the same and if so, she has to be careful; she couldn't admit how Sophie's mocking dismissal had been almost impossible to sit through. If they sense how easily she is thrown by their disapproval, how afterwards, she'd started to pack her bags for the trip home, they'd all take that tack.

"Suddenly, you're disappearing to Charleston with not a word to any of us!" Sophie had accused in their one phone call. "What the hell are we supposed to think? Except that maybe you're paving the way for us all to be prepared for the holidays next year? So the kids can get used to Grandma not pulling off her usual Christmas magic? No, now their surprise will be only this, you don't show up at all."

Bree had flinched, hearing the words. She knows her daughter well, her relentless lawyerly style. If she was going to hear an honest critique, she was going to hear it from Sophie.

"Sophie, please."

"Or what, Mom? None of this is normal! Dad's worried that the meds are making you act this way. I think he's right."

Suddenly, she's hearing static as Corey moves with his cellphone through rooms she can't see.

"Corey?" she demands.

"Um hmm," comes back clear.

"I want to say I appreciate you're not pushing me."

"All right."

"Maybe I haven't explained myself well. But it's not just the cancer these days. It's also these memories I've been having."

"Don't feel you have to explain, Mom," he interrupts and she wonders if he's even heard. Still, Bree knows it doesn't matter; she isn't able to offer much to anyone who asks. She doesn't understand herself why these memories seem to consume her. Instead she wants to steer both Sophie and Corey to their father, the psychologist. He can at least explain to them why she's acting so curiously, why sick people sometimes act in hurtful ways with people they love.

So I'm sorry, my babies. This time, she's not the one who can provide any answers. Even if they rarely seek out her advice these days, she needs to make them understand: she can't pull any more reassurances from a bag of tricks, or fictions either. Today, she has nothing left to give.

~13~

Research Shows Cancer Patients Often Suffer From PTSD

CHARLOTTE, N.C. Researchers at Columbia-Stevens Hospital have recently identified symptoms associated with post-traumatic stress disorder (PTSD) in cancer survivors. Their study confirms earlier findings released last year by the Taylor Cancer Institute in Durham.

Over the past two years, multiple studies have confirmed some patients may display symptoms of PTSD after receiving diagnoses of initial or recurrent cancer. Here in North Carolina, university studies now report cancer survivors can exhibit symptoms tied to PTSD even years after an initial diagnosis is given.

Post-traumatic stress disorder can be characterized as changes in behavior or thoughts following one or more traumatic experiences. Symptoms can include: emotional numbing, hyper-vigilance, depression, flashbacks, avoidance behaviors, and/or hyper-arousal.

According to Dr. Tim Laneer, a trauma specialist at Columbia-Stevens Hospital, "When cancer patients exhibit signs of PTSD, it is imperative they are further assessed for this disorder. And if it is determined they are suffering from PTSD, their therapeutic treatment should be viewed as time-sensitive and a high priority alongside any cancer care."

"To further complicate our understanding," Dr. Laneer adds, "Cancer patients can often become depressed or anxious over the course of their treatment. Doctors will routinely work to alleviate these pressures, yet fail to consider these symptoms may also be presenting as part of a trauma diagnosis."

In the North Carolina studies, researchers studied cancer patients diagnosed with PTSD alongside control groups of cancer patients identified as suffering from depression or anxiety, but not PTSD, so they might understand how similar behaviors can lead to mistaken diagnoses.

In medical communities, it is now generally accepted that cancer patients ranging from children to adults may experience symptoms of PTSD tied to their care. Dr. Laneer explains an initial cancer diagnosis is often itself the trigger for a PTSD-related episode. As well, patients receiving news of a cancer's recurrence may describe its return or the increased likelihood of poor outcomes as severely traumatizing.

In other groups of patients, initial traumatic responses to their cancer can also trigger an onslaught of memories that may be completely unrelated to their latest health challenge and should be treated as such. These patients may receive a slightly different PTSD diagnosis tied to their suffering that is not termed 'acute', but rather 'complex' or C-PTSD.

"Once cancer patients are diagnosed as additionally suffering from either acute or complex PTSD, trauma therapy can begin," said Dr. Susan Cole, a Dallas, TX family practitioner. "Mental health specialists and oncologists can be brought together and treatment plans can be aligned to insure each patient is receiving optimal care on multiple fronts."

~14~

Sure, he knew the history. Bree's parents had divorced in their later years after the death of the father's mistress, a neighbor next door. The decades-long surreptitious affair Dennis Overton had with Therese Rupin had nevertheless acceded to morality of the era and the Overton's Catholic ways. Nothing was ever admitted. Passions simmered quietly between the hedges for years.

Also, the mother's car accident had caused all members of that family to act out their own perverse resentments in barely detectable ways; no psychologist could ignore the chronology. William was sure Bree's parents had emotionally damaged each daughter during her formative years, whether by intention or simple neglect. He knew most grafts on Bree's family tree came up as poisonous, but he had never gone there with her. He wouldn't. Maybe there was more to mine, but he feared where too much knowledge would take him or Bree in regard to his in-laws; the impotent fury they might both suffer being unable to demand apologies from those no doubt guilty, but also quite dead. Instead he'd convinced himself that Bree had to some extent survived a dysfunctional upbringing by taking refuge in her own decades-long and healthy marriage.

However Bree had now left her home, seeding her departure with the same confused regrets as her father and in ways that reminded William too keenly of her ugly inheritance. Strangely, though, her family history also put some sense to Bree's abandonment; it reassures. For as long as William the psychologist can see flight as a learned behavior in the Overton clan, he isn't merely playing the part of husband in this scenario.

And so he's not stuck with only one theory, just one and no options: that he is the sole reason she's fled.

Dr. Sands stares him down as he takes a seat. His weary expression rips through one layer of embarrassment William has been feeling, to many others, without apology.

The oncologist then raises a hand to his cheek and starts rubbing, as if to tamp down pain or fatigue.

"So you're saying she left you without warning. But then you should know she did have the presence of mind to check in with me. I was able to help her understand the possible effects of traveling alone, medication alerts, and she seemed willing to listen." He pauses then adds, "You know, William, many of my terminal patients who choose not to pursue treatment beyond palliative care are actually quite realistically assessing their odds. They can face what's coming, often with far more courage than the rest of us. If that's what this is all about we've got to respect Bree's wishes."

What William is hearing is familiar enough; this is the sympathetic lecture. But he has no reason to argue with Sands. And what other choice does he have anyway when Bree has asked this specialist over his own counsel to help her navigate the trip? At the least, he will need to form some kind of alliance with Sands to insure his wife is safe, one that doesn't violate their doctor-patient confidentiality.

"Look, I understand what you're going through," Dr. Sands continues. "I'll urge her to call you if I talk to her.

Meanwhile, all my resources are open to you. But I suspect she'll be in touch with you before she calls here again, I really do."

"Please. She left for no reason I know, and now I'm worried her medications might be responsible for this sudden erratic behavior."

Sands' left eyelid twitches, just a shade, and William guesses what the doctor has the courtesy not to say aloud, *but wives leave their husbands all the time. That's not proof of crazy.*

"Look, wait here. I'm going to go tell my nurses to put any calls from her through immediately, no matter when they come."

If only momentarily, the two men trade glances as men, husbands, professionals. But then the doctor returns Bree's pink file to its folder, clamping down with rubber bands on the bulge. He straightens the collared folds of his jacket as if preparing himself for his next appointment and then he leaves the room. William is tired enough to ignore any obvious signs their meeting had concluded. He makes no move to follow Sands down the hall for a quick handshake and goodbye.

On Sands' desk lies a form, *Hospice Directives*, and words scribbled along a margin, *The patient is actively dying.* Not Bree's name, thank God. No, nor anyone's name visible which possibly saves William from any ethical line he fears he might be crossing.

But someone, some patient, is actively dying. Those words throw him more than he can fully understand. You actively die. You set out on that course from somewhere deep within. And here's an admission from the rest of us, a confession of failure really—we don't know where you're going. We can't follow. We can't help once you turn a certain bend. *Don't go.*

Absent Sand's notation on this particular patient, the form reads as a generic list of instructions on hospice care for the newly admitted. However, it also seems to be talking just to him, explaining things he never knew before.

When William's done reading, his heart starts bumping like a newborn, his own firstborn's thump on his shoulder. For a moment he fears he is having an attack himself. It is not a heart attack, though, but the opposite. It's a heart's consolation around one great truth.

We actively die. The body wants death at some point more than life and then there is no arguing. There is only escorting.

So as doctors, we become the best kind of escorts, truly humble attendants. For the doctor is no longer intent on debating with God over the patient's fate on the operating table or in counseling sessions. No, this patient is actively dying. Therefore, the only job of a good escort is to allow that patient to turn to death so that he should not dread or fear but prepare for the moment his untethered soul will have to face all of this, alone.

Short of that moment, though, let us travel with him as far as we can. Even if we must shift into other roles as teacher, coach, to set the pace, cheer him on.

This time we need to simply come alongside and not as trained experts, but as novices offering up our best medicine for healing, a steady smile, a grazing touch…

Until we are the ones losing our footing, struggling to keep up.

And then yes. We'll let them go.

~15~

No work today. William Durning has a different agenda.

He passes through the den where Bree has laid down what she called a Zen rock garden; in reality, the garden is little more than a slate frame that holds white sand and grey pebbles bought from a Macy's catalogue. She has set the arrangement on a glass tabletop and coming close, William can see a Lilliputian-sized rake and broom lying on their sides in the sand. "What we're supposed to do with these," she once explained, "is anything we want. No rules. Just let your mood inspire you."

"Sure," he'd replied, knowing well the Eastern philosophy of mindfulness. But he never really did more than poke up rocks then bury them; more than once, he'd been turned off when each tentative scratch of the rake across slate seemed to set off violent sand eruptions.

So it did stop him short when he glanced at this garden and saw what Bree had possibly left behind as a second note to him, maybe a clue as to why all these events had occurred. The largest of five or six scattered rocks had been set aside to sit in a glorious, isolated patch of grey slate. Most of the sand and other rocks had been swept to the four corners of the frame. So has her unhappiness been on display, in plain sight, all along? It's hard to know if he's missed warnings or is simply unaware.

Anger comes up, unbearable now. He heads into the guestroom to retrieve his rolling bag from the closet. He is going. No matter what she wants, he will find her. He opens the closet where they store the luggage, and it takes him only seconds to register the obvious; only one here, see? She has the other. She's gone.

As he jerks up the handle on the remaining bag, he tells himself he can't possibly understand her note, won't. They'd spoken only once in the forty or so hours since she'd left and now she wasn't taking his calls or messages. So those words she'd penned were proving a lie, *trust me trust*, and why? What was Bree's real goal? To simply get away, leave him, or be left alone with her secrets? In all the scenarios he's imagined she seems to need something, anything, more than she needs to be in this marriage.

William pulls the traveling bag onto the planked flooring in defiance of Bree's admonitions to pick up the wheels or they'll scar the wood. Who cares if they do and yes, he's feeling petty and as self-pitying as any of his patients today. Yet this anger also feels righteous and buried away for too long.

Bree doesn't even realize how good he is, how much he is willing to take on her pains as his own. Only one time before had he even been tempted to defy Bree outright, forget he had a wife at least for a few hours. He'd had his chance with another woman. Not a patient, nurse, or colleague's wife—attraction to any of these types would've been career suicide. No, William had made the smarter choice. He'd looked to a gal who tended the aquariums in his office.

The firm's partners had decided to put a fish tank in the waiting room; Drew Manning often regaled them with descriptions of a saltwater tank at an Indian take-out place that seemed to enchant all its customers, including him. The experiment with a tank in their office, however, left goggle-shaped trails of sludge threading up from a pebbled bottom. Patients complained of a vile smell.

The pet store was called, and a staffer sent over to fix the problem. A small-muscled brunette wearing camouflage shorts that blended with her tan lines arrived at the office after hours, and William still couldn't be sure what made him itch once they'd met.

"You know, there are just so many, you find yourself paying attention to all of them at the same time," she explained to her audience as she worked. "After the guppies are born, you're trying to get as many scooped into your net as you can. Meanwhile the Papa's coming up behind and he's hungry, he's ready to eat his young. You have to work quickly to save them."

The young woman's lectures on guppy fathers cannibalizing their young somehow had a strange, exhilarating effect on William. He watched her scoop from the aquarium for a good twenty minutes and couldn't focus on anything but images of those guppy fathers digesting, or how this girl's mouth seemed to grow wide and sloppy too. Only when she started muttering about a filter clog did William decide to close down the entire operation. He demanded a return and a full refund, but offered to help her if she moved everything back to the store that night.

Together, they managed to haul a now emptied aquarium into the back of her van. Splashes of tank water stank up his shirt but as grimy as he was feeling, he nonetheless decided to make the grand offer of riding back with her to *Critters Alike* to unload. He didn't think how he'd get back to the office without his car, didn't much care. But when she left the van and moved to the back to dig up three lidded buckets holding the fish, William put lie to his own spontaneity. He sat up front wrestling with a broken seatbelt feeling hopelessly ensnared, and not just near his groin.

The inside of *Critters Alike* had the caved look of any pet store. Half the overhead lights were turned off to cool down the inventory. In contrast, fluorescent purple lighting glowed like a Vegas hotspot in the reptilian section. The bathroom, however, couldn't have been a cleaner or more inviting place. It smelled like jasmine and sported a large shower/steam alongside the sink and toilet.

With talk between them of lower species exhausted, the girl shed her shirt and turning to the shower, invited him to join. William felt the boner of a man ten years younger and why not? But he didn't. In the end, he didn't and that was that. The smells of ferrets and sawdust and chlorine followed him out of that bathroom; he left the store with the same feelings of wistful regret anyone feels in a pet store when he wants to buy a handful of some purring creature, but can't.

William caught a taxi at the corner, a lucky break, even if the cabbie griped about his stink. He rode back to his office to retrieve his car from the lot then drove home. Settling into the nightly routines of the household, he kissed both children as they did their homework at the kitchen table. Nonetheless his wife didn't seem much impressed with this solicitous nod to domestic bliss. "They need to do their homework," she merely said while heading downstairs to do laundry. Feeling snubbed and so somehow rightly aggrieved, he'd retreated to the day's mail and bitched out of all proportion about the electric bill. Finally, she took the bait, yelling at him so harshly he had his excuse to take the kids (but not Bree) to McDonalds for dinner.

He'd bought them all supersize fries. Bree wouldn't have liked that, but just this once he didn't care. As William and his tow-haired offspring sat happily stuffing greasy fries into their mouths, he took stock of his revenge; he'd satisfied his hunger and theirs too. For he is a psychologist. He knows what people need and want is sometimes the same. That's why pursuits can't be denied. He planned to tell his wife all he'd figured out when they got home— "These are the big truths people live by, Bree!"—figuring it would be up to her to buy in or not. But by then, she was already in bed.

Now years later, he is heading to the airport, ticket in hand, and pretty much the same script in his head.

This time, however, she is going to hear it all.

~16~

This afternoon, Bree visits a decorative arts museum
just two blocks from her hotel. It is nearly four when
she arrives, but the museum is all but empty at this hour
and she doesn't feel rushed. Right off, she finds herself
wandering into a room that's filled with 18th century
portrait miniatures painted on ivory. Faces of both young
and older women hang in ebony frames along the walls,
all looking stiff in their jeweled neckwear. Some men are
portrayed too and in their stylized renderings, sport heavy
brows and wigs (thanks to chemo, Bree knows that weight
too).

Another century, this crew. Presumably, the top
echelons of Charleston society were arrayed for her
inspection even if wall signs only offered up their names.
These people were probably once aristocrats who could
afford portraits put forth on coveted ivory; some may
have been slave-owners, others supplicants, still others
ambitious doyennes.

As Bree stares at each in turn, she tries to take their
measure. Only painted eyes glint back at her, no glances
care to consider her presence. Nonetheless, she can
somehow see her future in these unblinking stares. If
they had understood the irony—that their audience
would be a dying woman soon to be forgotten by all but
a small handful of people on this earth—would they
have bothered to sit for days in their corsets, draped their

faces in arsenic-laced powders? While posing for all those painful hours, could they have imagined someone like Bree would be their future admirer? *Bree, we once paid artists to be depicted as larger, grander, than our own mortal frames. How are you preparing for your end?*

For the briefest instant, her chest seems to fill with more than the usual fatigue. Her glance travels across the room but she's not sure what she's looking for. These ivory portraits amassed in this museum: these people had come and gone, been memorialized. They'd been intent on leaving behind their portraits, their names, so that generations later, strangers might yet stare them down and note their last defiant claim; *You can't forget us. We're still here.*

So what can she think? Thank God for Charleston's elite. For they are still here, beating back centuries. All of them are lined up in peacock colors offering over triumphant smiles, a parade's worth. They provide clues on how to be remembered long after the body is gone. And soon Bree will be in that parade too, soon enough.

Yet now she is the one breathing and taking them in; she is the one shaking out a cramp in her leg as she shifts her weight. She is alone with them all but for a security guard checking in on her every ten minutes or so. And even he seems deferential to her unique circumstance, nodding as he passes by.

Most of all, she is alive. For the first time in a long time, she is luxuriating in each breath, she is confident in this place. She is the one leading, she moves.

While in this room, death is the one looking on.

~17~

William is not a queasy traveler and he enjoys the solitude of most journeys. Ironically, peace comes quickest for him at thirty thousand feet, especially if travelers sitting alongside don't ask him what he does for a living. When they do, he hides behind a book and waits for Bree to step in. As a psychologist, he normally resents any conversations off the clock.

In contrast, his wife is willing to give strangers all the time in the world to tell their stories. She will appear patient, understanding, even if later she may amuse him in private by mimicking a particular stranger's accent. She is particularly harsh on the Midwest twangs, but oddly tone deaf to the long slurred rrrs of fellow East Coasters.

Today though, Bree isn't around to protect him from a thin-faced architect who smells of a women's brand of perfume and complains about zoning board restrictions on one of his pet projects, a synagogue. "Can you believe there are still anti-Semites in this country?" he rages. William is amazed and not because one stranger was being so frank with another (as a psychologist, he is used to such desperate bids for attention). No, only this: after a two-minute eyeballing, this man had decided he could share his news with a fellow Jew. William surely hadn't revealed his religious views and these days he doesn't own up to being anything other than a Humanist. Nonetheless, the grey-flecked brow and eroding chin line he'd inherited from his father have betrayed him.

So yes, he is feeling vulnerable on all fronts. His father has been dead for years, but William can summon him forth in seconds with not a detail missed; those eyes circled in perpetual fatigue, dress shirts wrinkled in formations that seemingly mapped out every mile of the sales calls he'd tracked down that week. All this is part and parcel of his DNA too, there's no denying. And perhaps it's time for William to accept at least some of this baggage is his to claim beyond the physical; there's no doubt he's carried the old man's worst habits of stubbornness, reticence, into their home, to Bree's great dismay. What we never wanted to be in this life, we nonetheless become: all of us, all of us. What we do next, though, decides our path; will we carry or offload?

As a child he'd hardly known any world besides Brooklyn. His parents had never displayed any urges to travel beyond the sales trips his father routinely made up and down the coast. Then his family's world had been small as a lidded jar, with seven-block walks to and from temple every Sabbath, nothing more.

A person doesn't need much in life to get by, his mother had taught him back then. So before you go to bed, William, count out your wishes for three things. A handful of grapes, a newly laundered shirt, maybe a rock made slick after a rain. You can make yourself quite a world by imagining all two outstretched hands can possibly hold. In this way, you can always build a universe out of whatever is small and precious and catches your eye. For as long as you live, you can play such a game.

The few trips the Durning family did take together were strictly on the East Coast, their parameters running no farther than states near New York's borders. Once, his parents had taken him to Washington D.C., where his father was expected at a sales convention. While the entire family toured the city by day, his dad left them behind at night. With little to do, his mother had retrieved a butter knife from room service, and they'd whittled. Everyone had oohed and ahhed over his ridiculous portrayal of the sixteenth President on a bar of lavender soap.

Another time, William and his father traveled by train all the way to Boston's Fenway Park to celebrate his 10th birthday, but sadly the trip didn't play out as either might've wished. In an uncharacteristic display of extravagance, his father had urged on William all the burgers and hotdogs he desired. But the boy from Brooklyn froze when asked whether he wanted ketchup and mustard on his hot dog. He'd never heard of such a thing in New York, ketchup on hot dogs! Ready for anything on this extraordinary day, he said, "yes" to both if only to see his father's approving grin. Sadly, he became sick in a vast public bathroom afterwards and leaned against the wall in misery as men came in to unzip their pants, spit and not flush, show him their backs like trees while loose squares of toilet paper spread underfoot.

In the decades since, William and Bree decided to trade in the small worldviews of their childhoods for another: *See the world, you've earned the right. Get a bigger map in your head.* Travel wrapped around that promise. Bree had wanted to go see Paris, Dublin, Vancouver, Toronto; they had. They'd headed to Barbados for two years in a row, liking it so much. William could still recall the unexpected chorus of frog welcomes when they left the shuttle bus to enter their pinkly lit hotel. Cheerup, cheerup, the frogs sang as official Barbados ambassadors of cheer (compared to their

115

uglier, meatier American cousins who only played bass low in the throat). Cheerup, cheerup.

Bree had been lighter then, not just physically, but in every way. After the children were born, travel allowed them to view each other as lovers again, fall into those familiar tunneling gazes. So yes. Straddle the world; feel powerful with every step. While we are able, we will work hard to afford these vacations, pursue joy. And at least, we'll know this feeling in our lives—every inch we tread on this earth matters completely.

The heat is thick as a towel in Charleston, adding to William's confusion. He calls her from the rental car even as he wonders what to say. But "Please," is the only word he manages when she picks up.

"Don't," she says.

"What if I told you I was close?"

"I would hate you for the disrespect."

"C'mon, Bree."

"Why test me? Why test this?"

By this, what does Bree mean? He tries to concentrate on her next words.

"If I open my door, I don't want to see you. It would be—."

"It would be?" he repeats, trying to draw her out.

"You know. It's just—just."

Just. When a word unravels like a needle skipping on a record groove, that's truth speaking, and you're obliged to hear.

~18~

"You came anyway," she says first.

"Anyway. Right."

She considers this and raises a hand to her lips as if to shut down her next remark. Yet she also steps away from the door. He notices she's in street clothes, black pants and a flowered shirt. Also, she's barefoot.

He walks into a suite much bigger than the single room he's booked a floor below (all they had). Two queen-size beds sit in one room. Bree also has a sitting room, bath, a kitchenette complete with table and chairs. Despite the ample space, William sees few signs Bree has allowed herself to spread out and relax.

"It's not the marriage, it's not you," she announces.

She moves closer until William can smell her brand of soap. Her skin touches his where he is cool. Then Bree leans in and kisses him. Briefly, but deep, deep. Lips then tongue. Exploring by snorkeling.

When they step apart, she seems flushed by her own impulse.

Meanwhile William is a bit startled himself, registering for the first time that Bree's blonde hair has been styled in a new way. Before she started chemo this second time, his wife had opted for a short, short cut just below the ears. Today, she has used some kind of gel or maybe just water to slick down her hair. It is a more vulnerable look for her, every strand close to the scalp and the ravages of thinning hair clearly visible.

She hitches up her pants with one hand while her left foot goes on a blind search for sandals in her closet.

"Sophie, she's furious with me," she tells him, avoiding his stare. "She doesn't see why I'm here either. Totally takes your side."

He's a bit surprised. "She hasn't called me to say."

Bree looks up. "She hasn't?"

"No. I didn't know I could count on her as an ally. How about Corey?"

"Oh Corey, I had a normal conversation with him. Sophie, she's too much like you, William. You don't give her what she wants, she's pouting."

The edge in her words riles, despite his best efforts. "Is that how you think of me?"

"I didn't mean—," she says, her voice raw. "Forget it."

Still searching for sandals, Bree squats to rummage through the closet. This choice seems to require all her attention; William is forced to wait until she addresses him once more.

"Nobody knows I'm sick down here," she confides. "Nobody cares. I don't have to think all day about things I don't remotely care about."

"Well good. But I'm being punished for caring anyway, right?"

It is not what he means to say, but his heart's beating as fast as she is speaking and he's confused. He has not come here to lasso Bree to anything but their history, doesn't she realize?

He needs to tell her about the woman he loves and respects; the woman who prefers to move through this world anonymously and focus her attention on pet causes rather than selfish gains. Recordings for the Blind; baskets for shut-ins; visits delivering music and movie videos to restricted patients in the psychiatric ward of a hospital just miles away from their home. When she returned from those particular drop-offs, she'd urged him to call colleagues associated with the facility and complain. "Is it a joke?" she pressed. "To have striped carpeting laid down in a psych ward? Doesn't anyone see how that's a mocking?" She'd been right.

Or how she's raised their children. She'd bullied Sophie to study for her second bar exam so their self-doubting daughter would find her confidence and earn a passing grade; she'd been the only mom to chaperone "Bat Day" for Corey's fourth grade class at the zoo (although she confessed to William she'd also peed a little in her shorts gazing at those furred creatures and sat by herself on the bus ride home). Once she'd laughingly insisted she was going to give the kids a lesson in microeconomics and took them to a local fast food joint promoting a $100,000 giveaway, 'Just pull a sticker, win your prize!' She'd purchased 43 sodas and 37 bags of fries for Corey and Sophie, sat with them as they stuffed themselves and pulled at tabs. The entire haul resulted in three free sodas, nothing more. "That's what it means to live the odds!" she'd exclaimed, satisfied her lessons on "easy money" had been learned.

And yet, she loved beating the odds. She was the queen of scavenger hunts; their best days in those early years were spent treasure hunting through Manhattan's streets (and what better attic to pursue?) for the most incongruous items: a Bible with an orange cover, blue glass beads on a string, a sex magazine featuring an ad for second language learning (that had been one of their best hunts, William and Bree were kicked out of four drugstores that day).

Conversely, the presents she bestowed upon him were neither whimsical nor childish, but old soul gifts. She set up his dorm room at Columbia U. with a toaster, an electric can opener, a Navajo print rug picked up on Christopher Street which she then hauled onto the IRT. "I held the rug in one arm, hung on a pole with the other, and other passengers stared but no one offered me their seat," she chattered as she rolled out her gift in an extravagant sweep then proudly straightened to her full height to appraise the haul, opening and closing both fists until the blood flowed once more. Julius Caesar cozying up to Cleopatra couldn't have done better, he'd thought. Yet even then, Bree was laying down for him a blueprint of a marriage they could share. Offering him not merely a rug, but also a pledge to create a home anywhere they might find themselves in the future. For all his studies in advanced psychology, William did not then have the maturity to understand his girlfriend was herself a rare find. But he was lucky; she stuck around anyway.

He has come to say these things, but William doesn't know where to begin. Feeling wobbly in both legs, he moves to a chair and sits.

"I did imagine good endings for us," he admits. "I thought we had years to play out a clichéd script. Bike rides, movies marathons, walks at night by the water. Old folk stuff, I know."

"I might have wanted all that too," she answers back. "If I hadn't—."

"What?"

"Nothing. I don't know." Her mouth goes small. She gives up on shoes and pads over to the bed to sit too. "You're still too much in love with the ways we beat my cancer the first time."

"Bree," he says in flat response. "You're not even trying to fight back now. I'm terrified for us."

With this last confession, finally, he pushes her out of her stubborn rooting.

"It just feels like we're not on the same page," she cries. "I want palliative treatment, that's all. But you're in this—pursuit,"

"Pursuit."

"Maybe that's not the right word. But each day, you're watching me like some—."

"What?"

"Like you're my guard and I'm in prison. Like you can't keep your eyes off me."

"You're right, I can't," he's quick to agree. Yet now his eyes can only tear up, making her an indefinable blur.

~19~

"Follow me now. Just five years ago, two wars were being fought on two fronts," the T.V. Host is saying. "And where did we put our hearts or heads? Two wars, but few of us knew why Americans were fighting in either. There's no morality when our soldiers are still stationed in these two countries."

"That's the only morality," his Guest interrupts.

"Not if they don't understand the military's long-term goals. Shouldn't we have asked more questions, debated next steps?" the Host continues. "Given ourselves some kind of time to consider, 'Why are we still involved, is it worth it?' Should we have sent our soldiers to Iraq, Afghanistan, when the very populations they are charged with protecting are so hostile to their presence? And when they come back from their tours, Americans seem to have little interest hearing how our troops were spit on, shunned overseas. So many have returned now. What excuse do we have for effectively shutting down their voices here at home?"

William is watching the show with mild interest when there's a knock on the door. It's Bree.

"Keep your eyes on your show, I want to talk," she says, entering the room.

"You do?"

She gestures at the television. "So what's this?"

"Nothing important. I was looking for the weather."

William picks up the remote but Bree protests, "No, keep it on."

Without waiting for an invitation, she finds an orange chair and sits. William flicks the remote to mute and returns to the couch, thinking how his sick wife is nonetheless becoming quite the dictator.

As their glances meet, Bree regards him coolly.

"You probably want to know why I can't be with you," she says. "It's because I'm feeling your fear all the time."

He curbs his own need to say, *'That's in your head.'*

"Well, I'm sorry if I'm doing that."

"Oh of course, you're sorry," she snaps, and this new show of anger unnerves him.

"I didn't come down here to pressure you in any way," he manages. "But I won't give up being with you. I don't see how I can."

Usually he's the skeptic. Now she's the one squinting suspiciously as he sets forth his terms. She leans over and scratches at her knee, bunching up the green pants fabric. Both of her eyes are ringed underneath, he notices, but maybe he is only imagining the beginnings of a decline.

"If I can't convince you then turn up the sound," she says.

"The Pentagon continues to commit the American military to select missions in these war-torn regions," the Host is complaining. His tone commands attention and both William and Bree look to the screen. "Our volunteer troops are becoming drained. Don't let news of remote field weaponry being employed, drones and so on, confuse the issue. We're still stationing Americans in these regions and in some ways it is even more insidious to claim they're

123

not being sent to fight, only to monitor and advise. The rest of us are being lulled by distractions back home and are no longer tuned into the challenges these people face daily."

"It's all the same, lousy news. Not what you need to think about," William protests.

"No listen, he's scolding us. He's saying everyone turns the channel when the topic's disturbing and we shouldn't. Please."

She crumples like a child, pulls a pillow to her lap and strokes the fringe. William sighs and sits back. The screen has changed; no longer are they watching a live interview but a montage of soldiers patrolling in regions of Afghanistan, Iraq, more.

"Here's the good news," the Guest is saying off-camera. "As long as a soldier feels he or she is fighting for something important, he'll probably be okay. So if they're focused on their fellow soldiers or families back home, if they feel their work has value in any way, they have a good chance of making it through. It's only when erosion comes, that we see trouble."

"Erosion?" the Host echoes.

"An analogy, I'm making," the Guest replies as the camera pans back to the two in conversation. "When our troops complete a mission and survey all they have accomplished, instead of feeling satisfied, some may find themselves ashamed. Even in cases where they have performed admirably, they might be left beaten down physically, emotionally, much like the cursed King Sisyphus. Your viewers know the Greek myth of Sisyphus? He was punished by Zeus for his arrogance and condemned to push a tremendous boulder up a steep hill each day. Once he reached the top, he would be forced to watch that same boulder roll to the bottom. This went on every day, all his efforts proved futile. Ultimately, Sisyphus suffered most facing a future where nothing would ever change.

"Some of our troops risk falling into similar mental traps where they'll discount their contributions. They might patrol bombed-out streets daily in the cities of Afghanistan, Iraq, and seeing few signs of democratic advance they'll begin to think they've been fools setting new boundaries for tribal standoffs, nothing more. Yes, they will always serve the mission but tomorrow the same enemies always seem to return and attack, and those perceptions are valid; these wars have been waged for generations.

"Meanwhile here at home, we have begun to callously forget our American soldiers. We have started describing their time in service as merely a job like any other, with steady pay and generous benefits. When their unique sacrifices as peacekeepers are instead viewed as small and pedestrian, some veterans might descend into what I call a Sisyphean fatigue. I'd like to build on this metaphor if I might?"

The Host nods, "Go on."

"Our military personnel and their families should never be made to feel the sacrifices they make while serving our country are less than monumental. Unlike the doomed Sisyphus, they shouldn't think of their best efforts as irrelevant.

"The rest of us need to show we are deeply indebted to them for their time in service. And to do that, we must stop normalizing the combat experience as somehow akin to other job stresses. We must hear their monstrous stories; mourn their many losses. As long as the American public is happy to do otherwise, however, they are condemned to carry these burdens alone.

"As for me, I look about and all I see is a collective response to their pain that's so cavalier, so dismissive! Yes, we are grateful for their service. But those words mean nothing if we can't help them define themselves in new ways if they're looking to do so; at the least, we should provide them with those options.

"I'm saying these troops can step out of Sisyphean mindsets to reclaim their lives, but first we need to relieve them of their loads."

The Guest sits forward in his chair, clasps his hands. "I am not saying all our soldiers fall prey to this mindset. On the other hand, Americans should not be surprised by the steady uptick in numbers of U.S. military on active duty, also veterans, seeking treatment for mental illness. Or how many in each population attempt suicide daily, beyond the twenty or so who succeed."

William comes up blinking out of this rough talk. He hardly ever hears someone speaking this bluntly on the news without a partisan axe to grind.

Bree's reaction though, is even more pronounced: *she feels this.*

She must, because she's starting to shiver in that chair and her eyes are wet; she's crying.

William touches her knee, but she doesn't acknowledge him.

"Bree?" He prompts. "Hon?"

"Those vets. They've been trained to internalize their pain, take the hits so others won't have to," the Guest continues.

"When I'm working with them in therapy, they will often look to protect *me* from their pain. I sit and listen and sometimes I can almost see the grenades going off deep inside. I can't tell you how well they've learned to bury themselves while they're still alive.

"Even when they do finally share, these vets will attempt to shield me from the full weight of their revelations. Because yeah, they think their experiences were so personally damaging, they would prefer to stay mute and so protect others. Even though they may be desperate for their stories to be heard, they'll never ask. They'll simply wait for us to turn their way and notice the pain."

"I hope they can see there's strength in sharing," the Host says.

The Guest shakes his head and closes his eyes, leans forward.

"Usually, they have no desire to share what they've experienced, no matter the costs to their own mental or physical health. And why would they? Faced with the public's increasing disinterest in foreign engagements, they probably think they won't be believed. Or they might fear if they speak, they won't be understood. That all they lost or found out there will be reduced to no more than cheap stories swapped for drinks in bars.

"And so when I'm with my vets, we're both holding onto each other with our eyes… not even our words, because words would explode the room. We'd both be gone. We know this. And so just our glances are keeping us safe while we're together. We know this too.

"Then sometimes, I go further. I ask them, 'Can you possibly say any of it out loud? Give me that word, the picture in your head, so unspeakable but please, please, describe it to me. Show me how your world can pull anyone in.'

"You see, all I'm trying to do is circle the real arguments. Pluck them out of their dreams of lonely, what buries them alive. I'm telling them, 'Let's drag it all up from the dirt now, the depths of the sea. Let's fish for it, let's reel it in.' I'm trying to pull at least some of our peacekeepers onto shores where all is flat and calm."

The Guest rubs at the knees of his pants and coughs.

Bree is still crying. William can hear her breaths come up in erratic rhythms, hunh, hunh. As he stands and approaches her, she seems to tense. Her fingers grab at the pillow, yet she will not look his way. Anyone would say she's having an extreme reaction to the interview, but why? Is it possible Bree's conflating the traumas on the screen with those in her own life? William surely knows the signs. He's a psychologist, for Christ's sake.

"Bree, honey?" He tries again. It is only when she blinks his way that he corrals a breath. He clicks the remote to blacken the screen, then smiles at her puzzled reaction.

"How are you?" he asks.

Bree nods in an absent way. She asks for a drink. When she starts to push up from the chair to get it herself, he urges her to relax. He's ready to hover again, baby her.

He knows he's risking another quarrel, but this time, he doesn't care.

He finds a glass in a cabinet above the microwave and turns on the faucet.

So it's some kind of trauma they're dealing with now? PTSD?

Of course, she's been under unbearable stress since learning the cancer's returned. And yes, she's been depressed, anxious, but no more than he's found himself to be at unexpected moments. It's easy to acknowledge she's suffering in ways he can't imagine physically, but when it comes to the emotional strain—this blooming calyx that is stress, each feeling a petal in a paler and less distinct shade—he nonetheless has allowed himself to indulge in the irresponsible belief that they are both confronting similar torments.

As a husband facing the loss of a spouse, he can be forgiven for such delusions. But no therapist can embrace the same without being accused of malpractice. So stop confusing the two. Focus.

What does he know about PTSD in his experiences with patients? What doesn't he know?

While the water runs, he stares at a mosaic tile backsplash and has so much trouble following the design, he feels only anger building up within; a fierce impatience with this instinct to step back, be safe, get out of the way as that boulder falls.

He hears her again turn on the T.V. and calls out, "If we're going to watch more Bree, how 'bout something a little lighter?"

With every word, he tries to feign his own nonchalance, "Please, hon. Let's lose ourselves in something else, please."

.

~20~

They first met downtown, near Washington Square Park. It was one of those weekends between exams when a break was needed, and nothing cost less or promised more than a subway ride to the other end of Manhattan. Exiting at 4th Street, William had his first glimpse of Bree standing near the top of the stairs, as his roommate pushed him from behind to hurry along.

At street level, he was able to spot her again; she was part of a half-dozen or so young people handing out flyers to anyone they could find. Of course he was not yet aware of this girl's uncanny ability to stand out in any crowd, but she was definitely the long-legged blonde in culottes in this group. Her clothes were perhaps a risky choice in this particular neighborhood, but her smile denied any sexy intent, that smile shy. And William found himself attracted to more; this girl had imperfect, yet brilliant white teeth. When she approached him with an invitation, she turned her question into a statement and that cinched the deal.

"You're a student too, right?"

With barely disguised condescension, he had pointed to Roger as if to show her otherwise; made sure she understood so he wouldn't have to actually speak the words he was thinking, 'Not even close, we're on the doctorate track at Columbia and you're what, an undergrad at NYU?'

She didn't give him the opportunity to be so rude. Right away, she jumped in with her proposition, "Well, we're members of the theatre company here at NYU. We're staging a reading of our professor's one act play. He's authored it and needs an audience. I'll get credit bringing you in, but here's the catch. It's a reading right, you know what that is?"

She pushed strands of blonde hair off her face and William was charmed.

"What it is, you'll get a chance to change the script. I mean anyone in the audience can, if they make a good enough case. The playwright, that is, our professor, he's open to suggestions and we're having a talkback afterwards. So will you come and did I tell you? It's free."

It's free, she was inviting, and without much coin in their pockets, the roommates were tempted. William does remember thinking perhaps he didn't have a chance; this girl was working so hard and shamelessly to recruit anyone to the reading, not simply him alone. Besides, he imagined the professor had to be her god of the moment, her heart tragically laid out for someone skilled at exploiting stunning undergrads with little authority and probably less poetry.

Still, she'd drawn William into the semblance of a theatre off 8th Street, where hardback bridge chairs encircled a portion of floor taped off to suggest a stage. The professor's play struck William as a pretty contrived piece. But Bree did sit two seats away and that made up for much of the mediocre entertainment. While he feared he'd lost her afterwards to scattered applause and a huddle of students gathering round the playwright, Bree's height and that hay-blonde hair put her in his sights once more.

And only then did he realize—as he would for the rest of their lives—that getting close to her would take a bit of work. Bree held the center of the room; she was the climbing yellow pistil no matter how many others swirled round. To come alongside would be work. Worth it, always, but have no doubt. Work.

~21~

I'm sitting here, thinking of men of the cloth, he writes. Specifically, the priest your uncle sent us to see when we got engaged but begged off on Pre-Cana. How we never told him I was a Jew and practically agnostic, knocking on his door with a good Catholic girl like Bree Overton in tow.

Do you recall his advice, what he told us? "Save some money for what you'll need. Not just for anything you'll want to buy on a whim."

How angry you became when I asked a very reasonable question in reply, "Well, what amount do you think a young couple like us starting out might need?" A test for this man who'd taken a vow of poverty, but he didn't blink.

"These days?" he replied. "Five thousand seems like a reasonable sum. If you save that much together, you're laying a strong foundation."

Sound, sound advice, he scribbles. Cautious yet good-willed. But remember how we responded?

He wedges his missive under her door. She clicks open the lock a few minutes later.

"I remember his advice, yeah."

"Which we ignored," he's quick to remind her. "We wanted to get married, so why bother to be grown up about it? We were awfully arrogant in those days, Bree. Maybe we should come clean with our children, confess our awfulness. Then share with them all we've learned since."

135

Her nose wrinkles up playfully as she smiles. "Which is?"

"Whenever you can, please ignore good advice. We did fine spending our money on nonsense over the years. Life doesn't have to be what anyone else says, right Bree?"

As she leans on the door, it shifts forward.

"Come in," she says.

He enters her room in one stride, two, focused on changing all her impressions of him in this one visit. No more gloomy discussions or pigeoning stares.

"This doesn't have to be what Dr. Sands says, either," he says, pushing down worries he's overdoing it now with too much gee whizzing. "I mean maybe you're ill, but okay, you shouldn't have to automatically agree to treatments. Maybe I've been wrong about that."

She's clearly surprised and he's glad to see it. "You're not serious."

"I am. Forget Sands. Forget me too, insisting on anything you don't want. I mean it, Bree. We can go through the rest of our days together not even talking about you being sick. We can pretend the past weeks never happened, ignore warnings from well-meaning priests or shrinks or fortunetellers or oncologists. We can only look to each other and have faith it'll be all right."

She falls silent then murmurs, "Make-believe time."

"Yeah, that time."

Watching her, he can almost believe his own promise. She wants freedom so give it to her. And believe in each other, nothing else. No boundaries, no soothsayers, no calendars tracking their days to the next scheduled scan. Ignorance can be bliss. Life can be in a hotel room, pretending, and worlds can shrink, the whole universe can be as small and perfect as a gaze into a loved one's face. Who needs chemo hurls, straw hair, wasp-wing needles tamping infections?

"Unless the pain gets so bad you have to acknowledge it. You'll give me that?"

He doesn't blame her for the suspicious glance she casts his way. She knows when he is lying he will bite back a guilty smile so she is looking for it.

But then slowly she nods and William is heartened. From now on, he will be with Bree as he is with any patient who is willing to do the hard work. Those clients who enlarge themselves with their trust, who reinvent their world for fifty minutes every week and all he has to do is help with the edits.

So it can be in his marriage. The doctor can be the lover again, the man she longs for when crisis hits. And she's right; they need to forget the old healing rituals in the face of recurrence. Maybe if they can rule out all those time-consuming distractions, he can help Bree work through any traumas he now suspects are in play.

"We can stay in this hotel as long as you want, Bree. Or lease a rental down here if that's what you're looking for."

She allows him to step closer (he has finally figured it out, he has!) but then there's a knock on her door and they both turn.

"Who's that?" William says, checking his disappointment. "Did you order room service? I wish I'd known, I might've added to your——."

Heading to the door, he opens it to Claire. His sister-in-law stands in the hallway with a purple rolling bag propped up against her thigh.

"Bree?" Claire cries. "And Bill? Oh, Bill's here too?"

~22~

Claire enters the hotel room wearing black pants, a tan-colored shirt, and looking thin. William notes the gloss on her lips is unbecomingly pink and that her makeup makes her appear older than she is, regardless of any attempts to suggest otherwise.

Bree lets herself sink onto the bed. She makes herself small.

"Claire?" he demands.

"I invited her and I didn't think you—."

"When?"

"Before I knew you were coming," she says. "When you told me on the phone to call someone if I was planning to be down here awhile."

It is a peace offering, but he's unwilling to accept it.

"Really Bree? You honestly didn't think I'd come down here myself after we talked? I find that hard to believe."

"Yet here I am," Claire pipes in, her smile going crooked. "That's funny, huh?"

As she pulls reddish bangs off her face, she appears younger, more attractive. Nonetheless, William can hardly look at his sister-in-law. He's not sure who he should be angry with—Bree for wanting Claire, Claire for coming. Or himself, for being caught up short by his wife and again denied.

Claire moves into the space between beds with her rolling bag, appraising her choices. "Two queens?"

"I thought we could sleep in one room and save the money. We'll have more time together." Bree laughs as if she's trying hard to sell this idea, but Claire looks skeptical. "Or if you want, we could switch rooms for a king and a pullout. We have that choice on another floor, I've already checked."

Claire nods briefly then asks, "Is it a smoking floor, though? Oh never mind. I'm resolved to curb my bad habits around you for as long as I have to."

She turns to William and says, "I promise I'll only smoke out on the balcony when I can't stand it anymore. Does this room have a balcony at least?"

Bree points her in the right direction then watches as her sister rounds the corner until only rolling wheels on wood can be heard. She won't meet William's gaze, but it hardly matters. His wife has not invited him to share her room (much less her bed) since he's arrived, and he can't think of anything else.

Claire returns to drop her purse on the chair, the red bag unexpectedly camouflaging as a small creature against the flowery print.

"This is fine," her sister announces. "It's really a suite, isn't it? Plenty of room so we won't get squirrely with each other."

Bree gives them both a wide smile. "Well, good."

"And I'm happy to be here with you. But?" Claire glances over at William. "Am I missing something?"

"I don't know," he manages, pushing down the anger. "What do you say, Bree? Are you kicking me out?"

Bree eyes William steadily. Her mouth moves in small motions but she doesn't answer him. Instead, she turns to Claire and explains, "It's no problem, William's staying in another room. He didn't know that I invited you a week ago."

The rest of her sentence hangs in the silence: *while no one invited him.*

William inhales deeply. He does need to be taken seriously and so he can't argue his case in front of Claire. But his wife has to realize she's gone too far.

"Can we talk alone, Bree? In my room?"

When she nods, he tosses off, "We'll bring you up to speed in a few moments, Claire. Meanwhile, start unpacking and settle in."

She gives him one of her slanting smiles. A nervous biting habit has left its imprint, a tiny mark at the outer crest where her lips meet and part. Here, the reddening implies. Gravity.

"You're being awfully jealous," she says. "She's my sister, for God's sake."

"Why didn't you ask Eileen?"

"She's too much like you and Sophie. All she wants is to get me home and back in chemo. Probably if she thinks I'm getting the care I need she can check me off her to-do lists."

"That's not Eileen," he argues, disturbed to be thrown in with the others so easily. "Instead you want Claire?"

"She's blood, she's my sister. More than anyone else, she knows what I'm going through."

No, he can't understand why Bree is so certain and also so blind on the topic of Claire right now. But he doesn't allow himself to go down that path.

"Weren't we getting somewhere? Just give me some time——."

"I've told you and told you," she replies. Her face seems to pouch emptier with every word.

"Then I'm not listening well. Please."

"Soon there will be a hospice," she says with a groan. "Soon all I will have is a bed, IV drips, and you'll be changing me. Soon it's going to be this small and unthinkable world and I want to stop focusing on that."

Her glance rises to meet his.

"Help me ignore what we both know is coming. Let it all just somehow sneak up on me until this game's over and I can't do more. Please."

~23~

Only Claire might be able to clue in. Only her younger sister is brave enough to take on any threat in a fighter's stance, never show her fear.

Now and back then too, when they'd banded together against Aunt Syl's imperious rule; Bree was able to escape many of those confrontations but Claire had no such luck. With the older Overton girls off at school and their father eager to leave their invalid mother on any excuse, the toddler's daily care was assigned to two childlike adults willing to engage in ongoing, if inexplicable, combat with a three-year-old.

Years later, Claire would swear Aunt Syl terrorized her daily while rustling her up from her nap. "Why do you think your mother sent you here?" the angry woman would mutter during diaper changes. "Who wants to handle anyone forced up from her drugging?" For years, both girls had assumed their aunt was speaking out of school, griping about their mother's dependence on pain pills after the car crash. Only recently had Bree considered the woman might have been alluding to a different kind of incapacitation altogether.

On some weekends, Bree and Claire were sent together to Aunt Syl and Uncle Steve's house. The two quickly joined forces to confound these monstrous creatures willing to torture them for $1.50 an hour. They would sneak into their bedroom and opening their closets, spit into the bottoms of their aunt's slippers propped up on the shoetrees. When years later, the two sisters learned from the nuns that B.C.E. stood for "Before the Christian Era" and coincidently echoed their initials of Bree, Claire, Eileen, they marched about their relatives' house like Roman soldiers on a tear, clanging spoons on pots and chanting, "Before Christ comes again, we'll be saved! Before Christ! Before Christ!"

Away from the simmering stew of home, however, left alone by the adults to gloriously trample outside, the girls always laid down their quarrels with the world and instead offered up their mercy. They caught moths, tadpoles, caterpillars in cupping hands—but before the poor creatures could sense the darkness coming down and their worlds going black—they would free them, vowing to spare all innocents, always.

And so Claire is the natural choice, the only ally, who should be called in when someone is desperate for all kinds of mercy. Or was it only Bree who held onto such memories, needed them still?

Bree scratches her sleeve where it itches. She moves her glance off Claire's bag loaded with wrinkled t-shirts and denims to her sister's dress blouses hung in the closet.

"I'm grateful you came, don't think otherwise," she says.

"Of course, my sister wants me with her, I'll be there. God, this heat! It's like a sauna in here."

"Things okay at home?"

"Oh sure." Claire shrugs as she lifts another shirt from the pile, tries to shake out the wrinkles. "Since you're also a mother of two, you can imagine why I'd grab at any chance to get away, right?"

143

Then her expression changes as she turns her way; her face goes long and she admits, "Seriously, when I heard your cancer came back Bree, I cried for a week. I even went to church."

"Really?"

She laughs. "Well, not quite. I got as far as the parking lot. But I plugged in some of Daniela's stuff on my CD player and had myself a good selfish cry over you."

"What about the girls? Was it a problem to leave?"

Another shrug. "Daniela's old enough to be in charge after school and Trevor can step in while I'm gone. The girls understand you're my priority as long as you need me."

Hands on both hips, her sister studies her. Bree takes a few steps backwards and self-consciously tries to hide her body against the blind's striping shadows. They might have seen each other in New York only weeks before, but already her belly has swollen in a noticeable way. Tight waistbands in her pants confirm the shift. Another horrible irony of ovarian cancer is this: after you're gutted, your reproductive organs removed by the surgeons, you still must haul around the distended belly of a pregnant woman. Now Bree wakes each morning to feel the empty bloat of a stomach confused as to its purpose. It's as if school bullies have snatched away a lunch bag packed with healthy treats then tossed its contents, unthinkingly blown holes through its thin, papery remains.

Nonetheless, Claire offers up her verdict as she heads for the bathroom. "You look like you're holding up well. You're not in too much pain? Did you get your prescriptions filled before you left, or can you do that down here? What drugs are we talking about anyway?"

"Oh, they're serious," Bree murmurs. She feels slightly embarrassed, knowing Claire will soon find a zipped bag on the bathroom counter that exposes her stash. "You should've seen me at the airport. They're pulling me over, rooting through my luggage."

"Maybe I should teach you the tricks."

Another minute passes and Bree can dimly hear Claire clinking plastic pill bottles in the other room. "Oh, this one," she calls out. "Not bad, but I can't think this cures all your depression. Don't worry. I brought you some weed."

She wasn't expecting this. "You flew down with weed? That was idiotic."

Claire laughs. "Medical marijuana. Let them arrest me. Anyway it's legal in Colorado, and another state now, right?"

"We're not in Colorado."

"Fake cigarette packs, problem solved!" Claire calls out from behind the wall that separates them.

She exits the bathroom and reaches into her bag. "I was told you could get past security if you put fabric sheets in your luggage to take out the smell. It was good advice; it worked. You're sure you don't want some? It helps with the nausea, I promise."

Claire holds up her phony cigarette pack and taps its foiled bottom. She smiles like a cunning child as she offers a thinly rolled joint to Bree.

"I don't want to smoke with you, Claire! God. And whoever told you about this cigarette trick doesn't know what he's talking about. You're just lucky you weren't caught."

Claire shrugs then replies without a hint of injury, "Look, I know we're old ladies and all, but it's not wrong to smoke when you're sick. It's merciful. Weed's just as good and probably safer than any painkiller the doctors, your own husband, might prescribe."

"He's a psychologist, he can't," Bree mutters but Claire, holding onto her precious joint, doesn't seem to hear. Watching her, Bree feels fatigue wash over. Maybe William's right. Inviting Claire had been a mistake.

Feeling her irritation mount, she scolds, "If you're going to smoke, go back to the bathroom. Run the shower and put a towel against the door."

Claire cocks her head, smiling. "Really Bree, have one."

"Claire. Who knows what's in it?"

"Please."

She shoves the pack at her a second time and Bree decides to oblige her with a puff or two if only to stop her badgering. She leans over and pulls one of Claire's hand-rolled creations from the foil pack.

"Candy?" she exclaims.

Claire bursts out laughing. "Bubble gum! Did you really think I'd be such an idiot, Bree, to fly with pot? Daniela came up with it. 'Aunt Bree deserves a laugh,' she said. 'Tell her it was from me.' Come on, it's funny. I got you going, you have to admit."

Bree covers her mouth, but she can't help laughing. It is funny, this stupid set-up, even if it's on her. And she's thrilled Claire's come down here to lift her spirits.

"You did. Let Daniela know she succeeded beautifully."

"Yeah." Claire pops one of the cigarettes in her mouth, starts puffing small bursts of sugar. "See, I don't need to bring you pot. You're on stuff a lot stronger than anything

146

I could get my hands on. Although you might want to seriously consider weed as you go along, Bree. I have friends on prescriptions who still swear it helps the most."

Claire flops onto the sofa. She still holds her funny cigarettes between her lips, but she's no longer playing. Her expression's turned weary and dark.

"Really Bree, you're my guardian angel sister; my soul mate. It kills me you're going through this."

Bree can only offer up a weak smile. It's strange to be called Claire's soul mate but she's glad; maybe she made the right choice, after all. For she is so tired of being called heroic and admirable while she is anything but... Only Claire doesn't need her to be anyone but a sister, the frightened kid she's always been. Not a good fighter, not heroic, not any kind of martyred saint. Not stronger than goddamned cancer.

But William doesn't treat her like anyone but a capable woman with her own strong views, who's also his partner, his beloved.

She shakes off the thoughts and the accompanying twinge of guilt.

No.

With Claire's help she'll be able to sort through. She's the right choice, she is.

~24~

"Don't you dare not drink because I'm feeling lousy tonight and can't."

Claire grins. "That's never stopped me before. I'll have wine."

"I will too," William chimes in. He puts down his menu and while considering his next move, realizes he's spending far too much time watching the waiter adjust place settings. His sullen behavior's bound to raise all kinds of suspicions with Bree, but he doesn't much care. His wife should know he's feeling like the proverbial third wheel, the outcast, whenever they're together; she should be forced to live with his fury even as she continues to insist he's the one who's misinterpreted intentions at every turn.

Either way, she's trying to hide any preferences tonight. She's smiling, trying to start up conversations that center around topics of common interest. Sadly for her, there's few to choose from especially when any volatile words—children, family, plane tickets home—are thrown into the mix.

"I'm glad we could do this. I mean, start over with this dinner," she says.

"Like civilized folk," Claire agrees with a smirk.

"I'll admit maybe this wasn't my first plan, but here we are and I think that's fine. It's not like I'm mad at you, William. The more the merrier."

As she grabs a breadstick from the basket, Claire adds, "Yeah, you two had me worried silly when I first got here. But you seem okay now. So I'm fine with this truce, sis. All these years, I can't think William and me have spent any real time together anyway. Now we can."

For his part, William sips from his glass and doesn't say a word. As far as he is concerned, his marriage has stayed strong over the years because he's made a conscious effort to minimize contact with all his in-laws. He never knew Bree's mother as the woman died years before he met his future wife, and he's always been secretly grateful for that. From Bree's stories, he doesn't suspect they would've done well together. Still, her daughter had only been able to pay her tuition at NYU by digging into the trust fund her mother set up for all the girls, off multiple insurance settlements tied to her accident. He always has to give Mary Overton credit on that score.

After he'd heard Bree's stories of her father's desertion, he hadn't been impressed with him either. The two men only met a handful of times including the day he'd married Bree. Beyond those encounters, his entire relationship with his father-in-law consisted of the occasional swapping of stories over the phone. The man would call him to discuss final scores of baseball games and William would listen, even though he wasn't particularly a fan. He'd been assigned by Bree to sub in for his wife in those weekly conversations as she considered her father's decades-old affair with a neighbor an unforgiveable betrayal, couldn't bear even these innocuous exchanges. Instead, she and William had agreed one man's willingness to speak to another for ten minutes at a stretch seemed good enough for all concerned.

Dennis Overton hadn't lived to see his grandchildren and that was probably another blessing. While they did go out to New Jersey for the funeral, Bree made sure they'd taken a commuter train and a taxi to the funeral home. Only then would they have their excuse for a quick exit hours later; they couldn't stay or they'd miss the last train out.

Now he sets down his glass and watches his wife study him as he does so. Usually he's the one tracking her in his role of caretaker—are her eyes, skin, clear? Is a particularly long stretch of silence worth his probing? It's uncomfortable being the subject of her scrutiny now.

"You know, it's been a while since we've been so spontaneous, William," she says. "Both of us, I mean."

"I wonder why."

"I'm serious. It doesn't pay to constantly arrange our lives around my—,"

"Crap is the word," Claire offers.

Bree nods energetically. "Crap is the big C here, right."

"You know what I think, Breezy?" her sister chimes in. "Sorry, Bree. That you invited me down because we can always figure out ways to have fun in spite of crap."

"Sure, you're right."

"Also, you knew Bill would follow you down. I mean that was never a question. So what is it? Did you want him to learn from us how crap doesn't have to lead?"

William finds himself startled by Claire's insight, so unexpectedly on point. Claire seems impressed with herself too. But when Bree doesn't reply right away, her sister adds impatiently, "Yup, I think I've hit it on the head. What do you think William? Maybe I should've been the shrink, huh?"

150

"Maybe," he agrees, but really, he's been too long on the sidelines in this discussion. Time to regroup. "How 'bout it, Bree?"

"It's not like I'm trying to get rid of you, William," she says slowly. "I don't know what I was thinking when I left. All I knew was I couldn't figure out what I wanted from you or anyone back home. When I got down here, I wasn't as sure. But I thought it would be unfair to tell you so."

"Because—?"

"Because if I couldn't figure out what I was doing down here, it wasn't fair to string you along. Claire can freelance her graphics remotely. But your patients get frantic when you're away."

"That's what colleagues are for. They can take on my caseload when I'm not there," he grumbles.

Nonetheless, he can hear his tone soften in the wake of his wife's concession: *he'd been missed*. And bolstered by the plum-flavored wine, he decides to suddenly confide, "You want to know how easily my calendar can be cleared? I didn't come down here with any date set for my return."

"What? You bought a one-way ticket?"

"I did," he flips back. "How 'bout you?"

Bree opens her mouth as if to say something, then reconsiders. Instead, she retrieves her napkin from her lap and lays it on the table. "If I get up to go to the bathroom now, it doesn't mean I'm cutting you off, okay? It means I have to go. You two play nice without me," she says, still forcing the cheer.

Claire seems willing to do just that. The moment Bree leaves them, she confesses, "I swear I didn't know you'd be down here. If I did, I wouldn't have come. I mean, she asked and all, but three's always a crowd."

151

As for William, he's regretting everything he's spit up over the last few seconds. He is the reason Bree's mood shifted the moment he decided to impress the sisters with his own impulsive and feckless behavior.

"I'm not mad at you," he says, trying to shut down this sister-in-law. But she distracts him when he needs to regroup, when he must find ways to remind Bree this man at the table is still the reliable, competent partner she's come to adore.

Claire pauses then, as if silently debating the value of being seen as Bree's main confidante in this threesome. Finally, she says, "You know how Bree says the cancer's return makes her feel powerless? Like she's lost her ability to control anything? But look at her now, right? She's managed to control plenty getting us both down here."

In spite of his usual cautions with this sister, Claire brings him up short with this analysis; he's impressed. Perhaps he should reconsider her value while alliances are still being drawn.

"I'd say that's right. Maybe you should get that psychology degree."

She smiles again clearly flattered, and feeling more than a bit reckless, he confides, "Bree's been having these memories. They're churning up in her all the time and I'm worried."

He's startled when Claire's pupils slit thin as a cat's in response.

"What kind of memories?"

"She doesn't really go into detail."

"Then how do you know there's anything?"

"I've worked enough years as a therapist to suspect."

Her glance softens and she shrugs. "Maybe. Or maybe she's just feels she's on the losing side of this cancer and so she's taking stock of her life while she can, sharing everything while there's still time. I mean I hate to talk about this, because it means she's getting worse, right? But they say that starts to happen."

"She's not talking about me or the kids," he counters. "She only seems interested in the Overton girls, when you were all young. And your parents."

"Yeah?" Claire bats back. "Well what am I supposed to do?"

She turns from William abruptly and picks up a butter knife, trails its edge down the tablecloth.

"What do you mean? I'm not saying you should do anything."

"Good," she says, letting the knife fall flat. "Because I'm not playing any part in whatever's she's telling you. I didn't come down here to get into any of that. No thank you."

"I didn't mean she was expecting any stories would come from you—,"

"Because they won't!" Claire cried. "They didn't! If Bree starts with that shit, I promise you I'm on the next plane."

"Sure." Clearly he's floundering in his attempts to learn more of the family's secrets through Claire; on this topic, she's even more secretive than Bree. In a sudden shift of strategy, he decides to temper his tone as he would with a patient. For in the space of a few sentences, Claire has unexpectedly veered into that territory.

"We survived our parents. That's not some big news," she insists.

William doubts that claim but tries to offer up only a therapist's deadpan expression. How bad had it been

153

for the three girls? Maybe Bree is circling some pained truth the other two long ago decided to ignore or deny. Or perhaps only Eileen can make sense out of the chaos they'd lived through, the others being too young at the time. In any case, he has rarely heard any of the sisters bring up stories of their shared pasts except as disconnected narratives that seem to lose their purpose halfway through the telling.

"But boo hoo, everyone's got their stuff right?" Claire sniffs just as Bree returns to the table. "I bet you make a great living poking at your patients with all these questions."

"So what are we talking about?" Bree asks, taking her seat.

William shoots Claire a look that she pointedly ignores.

"We're comparing notes on you," she says. "What else?"

~25~

"Let's go to the movies."

"The movies?" Bree laughs. "Here we are in Charleston and you want to sit in the dark?"

"We'll have fun."

"I'd rather see the city by day," she grouses. "Or better yet, we can get something off the pay-per-view at the hotel."

In some ways, illness has really spoiled her. No matter what her sister may want, Bree expects her to fold. Instead, Claire surprises her by insisting, "We walk around this city all day and it's beautiful, I admit—but this heat! I'm not used to it. All day, I'm walking around wet. At least at the movies, there's air conditioning."

Who, except Claire, would dare to upstage the cancer patient with her own complaints? But she has always been the youngest, the spoiled one, she has no remorse.

So, they will swap out the oyster-damp kiss of Charleston's streets for a theatre's cooling embrace. Bree insists they walk there though, and at a turtle's pace. She can claim fatigue if challenged, but the truth is she adores this weather. Heat is what seasons north can no longer provide; only heat promises soothing memories alongside all the others.

For it had been summer, that season, when she'd enjoyed her first remission. They'd heard the news just weeks before Independence Day 2009. In the spirit of myth-making recovery, William and Bree had stretched mid-June's promising news well into August. Remission had marked their moment of triumph, so wrap it round and forget negativity everywhere, the wars in Iraq and Afghanistan, a rocky economic recovery. This year, Independence Day would be theirs to claim.

And so, on the fourth, they stood curbside watching a Main Street parade, reveling in every colorful character passing by. A high school band with the hoped-for Mickey Rooney flair; men wearing funny hats who drove miniature roadsters across flag-draped avenues and threw caramels on the pavement for children to eagerly pocket. Everyone waved flags like no tomorrow for who needs tomorrow? For some reason—the roadsters, the candy, the clap of cymbals or just maybe the shove of heat on their shoulders—both William and Bree completely bought into the corniness, the lie and promise of that day. Hope was not a whisper but a jubilant shout of victory: *We've won! We've won! We've won!*

We've won! But now she has come to understand the fine print of the deal they'd made: remission offered up in one glorious summer came with conditions and would not last many seasons. She had guessed at this truth, realized it months before William, and yet she hadn't breathed a word of her fears. How could she, after what they'd been through?

She said nothing; neither did William. Over the next years, mutual dread permeated their triumph most subtly. And Bree now fears their best attempts to battle a serious illness have become something else; a Quixotic farce where for too long they've peddled the lie that sheer, stubborn grit can transform a season; that birthdays of grandkids, Halloween, Thanksgiving, only flicker briefly when set against the brilliance of that long-awaited day. It will be Christmas soon.

Bree knows Claire's trying to time her fast clip to her sister's labored shuffle. She finesses the differences graciously by linking arms. Yet her sister also has a penchant for heels and as she attempts to keep her balance on the cobblestone street, she squeezes Bree tightly.

"Wait, you're hurting me," she protests.

"C'mon, don't you always say nothing will ever come between us?" Claire jokes even as she leans in.

"I do, yeah. Although the truth is we're living just a few train stops away back in New York, for the first time in how long? And still we hardly see each other," Bree snipes in a jab she regrets as soon as she hears these same thoughts spoken aloud.

Although Claire's eyes are hidden behind sunglasses, Bree can guess at her hurt. Sure enough, only seconds later she shakes her arm free and declares, "Yeah, it's weird we don't see each other more when we're home. But I don't have a car, remember? So it would be hard if I had to rely on train schedules, or maybe the buses. It would mean traveling all day—."

"You came when I called," Bree says quickly. "That makes up for everything."

To Bree's surprise, they don't talk much about the movie afterwards. She knows William wouldn't miss an opportunity to offer up his own detailed review but "worth the price of admission," is all Claire says before moving on.

Along King Street, mannequins sporting sunhats in a window display lure them into a shop. It's not much but Bree's at least willing to buy a hat for some protection on these iron-hot streets.

"As long as we're down here," Claire agrees and soon both women are rummaging through racks, pulling satin underwear from shelves. Her sister is so rude when a saleslady approaches ("You don't have what we're looking for? Why not?"), they are quickly abandoned and Bree finds herself playing a familiar role of handmaiden to her younger sister. But she doesn't mind this assignation; cleaning up after Claire has always been her job and realizing nothing's changed offers up the absurd possibility time may not actually move as fast as one might fear. As Claire pulls her choices off hooks willy-nilly, Bree's left contending with plenty of messes underfoot but, yes, she is also starting to enjoy herself.

"This is nice," her sister declares, while wrapping a print skirt inches too short around her waist. "Okay, you're being polite. What?"

"It's a little young," Bree demurs, then, "Are you buying for the girls too while you're here?"

Claire shrugs. "I don't know. They've got their own tastes. So I say they've got to use their own money. Look at this."

Her sister holds up a scarf decorated in a purple and red diamond pattern. Bree is drawn to it immediately.

"That's gorgeous," she agrees. "You know Carla, she cleans our house? She's been showing me all these ways to hide my thinning hair. She's brilliant draping these things."

"Then buy some," Claire urges. "There must be a dozen here, all different prints."

"Yeah, well. I already have a bunch at home."

"C'mon, go crazy. I'm the one who has to live off crumbs," her sister scolds even as she gathers clothes in both arms and heads for the dressing room.

Bree hesitates for a moment longer then loops the scarf back onto its rod. She follows Claire into the dressing room and waits on the other side of the door, listens to the click-click rhythms of hangers being dropped and retrieved.

"Daniela working?"

Despite her own self-pitying posture when it comes to finances, Claire doesn't seem at all hesitant to discuss her daughter's earnings. "She was, until she had a run-in with her boss. I told her, 'Go and make your apologies. Get that job back.' But Daniela's so quick to blame everyone else. It's never her."

"How bad has it been between you two lately?"

"She's a mess; not liking herself, not liking anyone. I tell her what's going on in my life, she says to me, 'You know Mom, all you've gone through, so have I.' She's pretty convincing until I remember she's seventeen and still living under my roof rent free."

She pushes the door open and stands before Bree shirtless, her freckled chest only partially covered by a bra showing its 32D tag. Still resembling an adolescent in this way, and never mind she claims two teenagers of her own.

"What about your kids? I'm guessing Sophie's been giving you a hard time?"

"We haven't talked much," Bree admits. "She's furious with me for leaving."

Claire shakes her head. "I don't mean is she angry, Bree. I mean, is she staying away from you because she's scared?"

159

"Scared? Why would she—?"

"Well." Claire scratches the back of her head, seemingly just as thrown by her sister's confusion as Bree herself. "Your cancer. I mean, it's *ovarian* cancer. They say a woman has a higher risk if there's a family history, isn't that right? If it is, you've got to assume she's scared. I know I am. How many times do I wake up thinking, hey poor Bree, but maybe also me?"

She glances over at her nervously, adds, "Look, I'm only saying this because we're all part of the same gene pool. The number's in for you now, but maybe soon it's Eileen or me. Or any of our girls."

Her sister's not crying exactly, but her eyes are bright. She seems to have frightened herself with her own candor; her mouth's half open as if she's ready to apologize.

And now it's Bree who wants to change the subject. Claire doesn't know what she's talking about. She only focuses on bleak outcomes. She knows this about her sister, so why keep listening? Only a masochist or crazy person would.

Still. Doctors won't say how sick you are, but your family will. Every time one of them looks your way.

Claire must've sensed her anger because she backtracks quickly, saying, "Look, I don't know what I'm talking about when it comes to Sophie. I'm probably just being stupid, forget it."

"You really think Sophie's spooked because I have this particular cancer?"

Her sister takes a breath, gives her what she needs. "No, Bree. Sophie's a lawyer, she knows how to do research. She's not going to be scared of anything. I'm the idiot here. Me."

She bends down to pick up a blouse she's dropped then says, "And don't worry about what anyone else is thinking, that's what you always do. Be selfish for once. You want to get away? Quit chemo? You do it. And don't let us throw our guilt trips on you, even me. You're the one who counts here, Bree."

Bree looks away, not wanting to see or hear anything except Claire giving her these reassurances. Repentance asked for, received. Besides, what else could anyone say that might hurt more?

If only to distract herself from having to think about anything her sister's implying, she drapes the plastic hanger she's holding atop a dressing room door and reaches for her purse, pulls out her wallet.

"Okay. This will make you happy," she says loudly. "I'm buying. Anything we decide on today is my gift to you."

"You're buying?" Claire cries. "Here I come down to take care of you, and you're mothering me?"

Here you come to frighten me with your what-ifs about my only daughter when you have two, but yes, Claire...

"I am," Bree assures, sensing even as she speaks this is no lie. If she can regain an advantage in this visit with no more than a healthy bank account, she will. It's easy enough to appease Claire in this way, she knows; to move her sister off all these dark and unsubstantiated thoughts she feels compelled to share as quickly as they flare up even while she ignores other truths: any tunneling air passage, any oxygen, only feeds those licking flames.

Besides, maybe miserable outcomes are all Claire knows. Why punish her sister for being brutally honest, horribly self-involved, when these are her habits? Nothing Claire does will ever surprise her. And maybe that's why she needs the youngest Overton sibling to stay close.

161

Bree knows she does best when she's in control of the caregiving. For years now, neither William nor their children have needed her as they once did. With Claire, though, it's easy enough to pick up a skirt or wet towel she's left behind on the bathroom floor. Even a cancer patient can tackle that to-do list and pass herself off as competent. Especially if no one's looking too hard and she knows Claire never will.

Yes, she can come up with plenty of other reasons to keep her sister near. And never mind if she has a hard time articulating them to William or Eileen or even herself. These days, her inability to logically think things through can be blamed on the meds she's on, doses that fog her brain as much as the chemo ever had.

In the end, Claire's the one person who knows the rules of their particular game by heart. Maybe that's all they've both come to expect from the other.

And maybe that's enough. It's as simple as that.

~26~

With her iPhone, Claire takes a few shots of Bree sitting directly opposite them in a chair. William notes his wife's in her usual graceful, if unconscious, pose; one leg hitched stork-like under the other.

His sister-in-law leans back on the couch they share and assures him, "I'll develop everything and send copies, I promise."

"Make dozens."

"Sure, I will," she yawns. "So, what are we here to talk about?"

William's wondering that himself. At the moment, Bree seems particularly nervous with Claire, certainly less confident than she'd acted with him just hours before. Then she had pushed him to fly back without her, claiming her sister could sub in if she suffered any health scare. She also assured him she was taking her meds religiously, following doctor's orders to the letter.

William wasn't sure which of her comments rattled him most, and which simply frustrated. It took all his strength to pretend these latest requests were similar in tone and substance to the hundreds, even thousands, of favors she'd asked him to carry out over the years. But he's decided to ignore every urge to call her bluff. And if Bree can convince him Claire's ready and willing to step up, do the work, he'll consider setting a date for his departure. Yes, he's reached that point.

Besides, he probably shouldn't be surprised by anything she asks these days. Hasn't Bree been laying down her terms in their marriage for months now? If she wasn't so sick, he'd feel nothing but contempt, shame, for all the ways he continues to accept the nonsense she dishes out, how he will fail to correct her even when he knows he should.

"I wanted William here so he could teach you all he knows about helping me," she says to her sister as he watches, amazed by Bree's willingness to be so generous with her compliments.

"But can't I just call William if something happens? He's close enough."

Bree shakes her head as if to dissuade her and William doesn't say a word. He knows such spite is petty, unattractive, but also his own to nurse for as long as he wishes. Bree can't control him on everything.

"Calling me won't be possible if I'm told to go," he does mutter in a loud enough voice for both to hear.

Bree shoots him a look then continues, "We're not talking about anything big. Just our daily routines."

"You mean if I'm out with you and William's not around?" Claire stipulates, seemingly not cluing into her increased importance as this husband and wife seek to pass off their routines. "Like when we were at the movies the other day?"

William's slightly surprised Bree's laying out the particulars of caregiving in such a disingenuous way to someone who needs to understand she will be on her own soon enough. But then he realizes: if she tells the truth, everyone bolts.

"Let me get you up to speed," he interrupts. Bree seems to immediately sense what he's up to and digs in.

164

"I was going to give her the specifics."

"But I'm the one who's actually gone through every drill."

Bree bites her lip then demurs, "Well okay. Then at least, can I sit in and hear what you tell her?"

A warning. Don't scare her off like a doctor might. Or worse, a jealous husband.

"Either way."

"I promise I'm not looking to second guess."

"I'm not accusing," he retorts, but his irritation finally bleeds through.

Bree ignores his petulant turn. She moves one of the couch's small pillows onto her lap and says, "Okay, I'm actually amused by this. Go ahead. Tell her what I like."

He smiles too, forces it. Then, "Give her decaf teas at night, even in this heat."

Claire raises a hand in salute. "Can do. Room service."

"Shoulder rubs when the pain gets bad."

He's surprised when Bree lifts her chin and winces. "Not anymore."

"No?"

"It hurts to get touched in the old places," she explains, and William feels he should've known.

"Foot rubs, though," he says weakly.

"Yeah, still the feet. If you can stand them."

With that warning, she unexpectedly pulls off her socks. Those heels are callused and white, as if she's walked through powder.

"Ew, disgusting Bree," Claire exclaims. "When did you give up on your old, great feet?"

"Good question," his wife says, leaning over to touch. Her tongue flashes pink between teeth as if she will allow her child within to deliver up the keenest appraisals; are they so disgusting, so gross?

Suddenly he feels defensive. It's true: they've strayed since her remission. During her first bout with cancer, they'd made ongoing commitments to healthy food and exercise regimens. But they'd both been so glad to get back to their lives when the scans came back clear. And so they'd forgotten the value of daily weigh-ins, foot rubs, unending care.

Claire notices where his glance has gone, teases, "Really, William. It's not like you to fall short."

"Is that right? So tell me, Claire. Do you know how to respond if ascites kick in?"

Her nose wrinkles in confusion. "What's ascites?"

"That's when fluids build up in her stomach. Bree's stomach might look bloated but she won't have any appetite, she might have trouble breathing, You might have to call a few doctors down here to find someone who's willing to drain."

"Drain her?"

"To relieve the pressure," he flips back. "But ascites is nothing compared to a possible blockage. That's life or death stuff right there."

He glances Claire's way and as she is starting to look uncomfortable on that couch, he's even more eager to share.

"Did Bree tell you what to do when her temperature spikes over 102°? Because at 104°, you're heading for urgent care."

"You'll have to give me instructions," is all she can say.

But, "No, he doesn't!"

It's Bree barging in, looking to take *him* down.

166

"He's trying to frighten you," she snaps, meeting his glance and not letting go. "I'm not anywhere near that level of incapacitation and won't be for a while."

"You're betting," he counters, but shifts his tone.

"Maybe. But if anything happens, we'll call my oncologist. We'll take a trip to one of Charleston's emergency rooms. I've checked, I bet you have too. One hospital's just minutes from here."

"Fine. Then let's get back to what Claire *can* do for you," William sniffs.

"Okay, Bill." Claire agrees, exhaling loudly. "But let's keep it light. Let's keep it clowny."

Clowny. That wasn't a word. And Bill. Bill isn't his name. William bridles, in spite of himself. Maybe he isn't what Bree needs to feel safe, but really? His wife has to see Claire may not be the right choice either.

So, no. He isn't proud of himself, but he goes there. "How are your kids doing while you're down here, Claire?"

Claire stirs on the couch, sensing he's crossed lines even if she's not sure how or why.

"Okay. Daniela, she's giving me some trouble."

"Yeah? Maybe I can help. Tough adolescents are my specialty."

"I've got things under control," she says in a low voice, clearly not trusting this turn in the conversation.

"What? I didn't hear."

"I said it's under control," Claire repeats as she pushes up from the couch. "I'll tell you this, though, I've been thinking of changing her school when I get back. You know, make a move."

"Why's that?" he prods.

"Well, I don't like who she's hanging with, for one," Claire replies.

But he's heard this same complaint how many times before in his sessions with patients? She's boring him now, he already doesn't care, and so nervously, fleetingly, he turns his attention back to his real target, Bree.

His wife's scratching her chin as she listens to Claire's problems with her daughter, she's looking less friendly on all counts. He studies her for a moment as if she is a stranger, this middle-aged, balding woman with her soft, swaying belly pushing beach ball-friendly at her shirt where it's buttoned. He studies her neck, once so smooth and long, stemming at the chin like some kind of glass-blown vase. That glass so pure but in some spots there's fog, a blurred peach patch, like the whisper of any secret cluing us in to all those places where the artist had paused to catch his breath while he worked. Now that neck he'd kissed, he'd stroked, is just as saggy-baggy. No passerby would look and think, 'Attractive,' anymore. No one would even think 'Healthy.'

But they would still have to stand back, make room for Bree in any crowd. They'd still glance her way and think, 'Tall.'

Maybe yes, he can regret how aggressively he's turned on Claire; she's an innocent party to all their intrigue. Still, his wife needs to understand what kind of irresponsible caretaker she'll have to rely on now that he's being reassigned.

And she has to know how much she has hurt him in their marriage too, for reasons that still aren't clear.

"You're the best husband I ever could have asked for," she'd told him just hours ago, but already stirred to anger, he hadn't heard those words as any kind of compliment. Rather, they seemed akin to send-offs someone might have penned in a letter back in the days when letters were written. Along with all those other well-meaning platitudes: *All love always. With Gratitude. Take care.*

~27~

Two nights ago, Claire had awakened her, calling out her name in a panic, "Bree!"

She'd startled awake only to find Claire sleeping peacefully in the next bed. Nothing offered up any clues to suggest the summons was real and the next day, Claire said much the same.

Nor could she figure out other odd thoughts she'd been having all week. Maybe the fine print on her pill containers held clues. Every pharmaceutical commercial on T.V. lists multiple cautions tied to use. Were delusions listed as possible side effects, also suicidal tendencies? If so, it's not her then, it's her drugs. Still, she needs to figure out which meds might be toying with her mind so viciously these days.

Not for the first time, she finds herself pissed at William for not taking the psychiatric track in school. He could've been so helpful telling her exactly what to keep or toss.

But of course, she can't look to William for help anymore now that she's made such a stink about him staying in Charleston. She practically told him to leave and she wasn't at all sure he wasn't offended. As for anyone else—Claire, Eileen, even Sophie or Corey—she knows better than to ask too much from people who want to help her but don't have the knowledge or skills.

Still. When the pain's seeping through and all her own, it's hard to be so magnanimous. *Or have patience with anyone who either can't help her, or absorb every hit as she does; who instead can escape all that's shitty or cramps. Or the burning as it comes up from her insides, and the smells of her now, the puke she leaves behind. All these really crappy pains of the Big C.*

Bree didn't used to curse much. But now she does, all the time. And it's not laziness with words, or stupidity, or even the drugs urging her on.

Instead you have to know by name the filth coming up in your mouth, your heart, you have to stare down all this shit and spit before it buries you alive.

And don't flinch at the sight of blood, that's what pussies do.

Pussies, there's a soft word that fights hard.

Or what else when the pain comes, what else?

Claire knows these words too. So tell her what you need. Ask your children. Ask your nieces.

But no, wait. Don't let any of them, Claire, William, Sophie, know what thoughts simmer inside or they'll make you go home. Back to your garden, your check-ins, your sedating lavender scents.

And Bree doesn't want prayers, or quiet chimes, or meditations this time. She doesn't want flowers to fight the weeds inside, no.
She only wants anything that can make a snaking knot unravel, a scream so loud the heart goes still: any of that, any of that.

~28~

She asks for juice and Claire responds, "You want juice, Bree? What kind?"

With one eye open, she watches her sister move to a small refrigerator in another room. A toy of a refrigerator: where were they?

"There's orange, tomato," Claire calls to her, opening the toy door. "But those aren't great, right? How 'bout this?"

She brings back a child-size cranberry juice box, the straw already poked through the hole. And Bree's suspicions can be confirmed; they're playing the same game of doctor as decades ago, only Bree has the starring role of sick baby this time round.

Claire's reddish curls calm her. She can usually find her sister anywhere off her hair color and that somewhat lazy walk. She knows it's her sister every time then, not someone else coming up to confuse her.

Her hair is as it's always been. Claire never needed to dye.

So stop looking so worried, sis. Bree isn't going to die either.

She's feeling lousy, hot and lousy, but can still come up with jokes to get everyone through.

Back then, their mother refused to call doctors no matter who was suffering. "We've had more than our fill," she'd say if anyone challenged her and after a while no one did. There'd be no credit given to the medical profession from Mary Overton; not to doctors or nurses, not in a single recounting of her accident or recovery.

Instead, she'd figured out her own alternative treatments to get by. Whenever Bree or her sisters took ill, their mother would go to the pantry to retrieve her palm-sized, most vile, brown bottle. She never revealed its contents to anyone so it remained an open question. However, simply holding that bottle calmed their mother like nothing else. With the softest touch then, she'd caress throats, roof foreheads with her hand, her palm flat and cool. "It's like she knew we were sick before we did," Claire would marvel years later, if grudgingly.

One, two drops worth; Bree couldn't remember any particular taste of the syrupy liquid but basing her memories on Claire's seemingly endless trips to the bathroom, she guessed it had to have been indigestible. Had their mother relied on castor oil, fish oil, some noxious mix? It was something healthful that purged anyway; every ache and sweat, also every doubt that their mother wasn't right there with them through the worst, stroking backs, balling tissues. "All those years you took care of me, but you shouldn't have—this is my job," she'd reassure. "To take care of you." And then she would put that hum in the air to sit alongside both parched and wet until sleep came, until the black inside their days began its relentless pour.

He's shaking out the pills she needs now, preparing a schedule for future doses. Just in case.

Don't worry, Claire. It's always just in case.

173

And is that their father standing near the door? Or William? Even as she comes up from her doze, Bree is pretty sure it's her husband. Claire's not acting any differently as she pads about. So there's another clue it can't be Dad.

"Bree, are you up? I think she's up," the man says. Maybe he says it twice, a dozen times, she can't keep track.

At the same time, she has seen her father looking just as helpless when people are ill. He will also stand at the door; he may push cone-shaped shadows of light into the room with the tip of his shoe, but he won't go further. Meanwhile, women and girls wander freely about these same rooms; spit rags slung across their shoulders, bobby pins holding back sweat-wet hair. They're ready to nurse; they all did, they still do.

Somehow she senses William has to be standing at the threshold because their father would never stick around for such a long period of time. Like Bree, he's taking in this scene; he's absorbing the hushes and rustles, the groans of this room. Uncharacteristically, he appears willing to be a spectator and not her caregiver, not Claire holding up a thermometer.

So maybe he is also the man she must impress with good health before she can leave this bed. Then she can join him at the doorway of this sick room, or any room, where people can come in but also head out. There's a choice and a hope promised under these wooden frames, these cracks of light offered up in the angled spaces so we might peek, see, but no more. There, Bree and the man can stand as two awkward sentries, neither willing to engage with her illness more than they can bear. And they shouldn't have to, they shouldn't. They've both done enough to help; she never seems to improve.

Remember standing at the door with your father, Bree? Looking in?

William may not know she is following him as he walks over to the bed, but she is; she sees all he sees in the very same ways. And what's in this room? A wife, her cheeks duck-like with bloat. Her shoulders jammed up against pillows, so where is her neck? This is the spouse he must tend to every time?

This woman is his wife?

Bree feels she must've stood in this same place for years, watching all that goes on in these rooms where people get sick, people heal.

She knows exactly how many steps she can take towards any bed before the dread kicks in.

~29~

"Not you!" Bree groans at him. "Go away!"

"Let me then." Claire pulls the top sheet from Bree's thighs where it's bagged, brings it up to lie across her chest.

"This is like dealing with Daniela when she's high as a kite," she says, stepping back.

"Just keep reminding yourself it's not personal," he mutters, realizing he might need to hear these reassurances more than Claire right now. "She's pushing through so much pain she doesn't know what she's saying. I talked to her doctor and he said to expect setbacks like this, especially if she's not getting enough rest. Plus, the drugs she's on give the most relief, but they also make her loopy. He wrote her some new prescriptions; there's a Walgreen's down the block. I'll get dressed and head over."

Claire wavers. "Shouldn't we be thinking about a hospital?"

"It depends how the next few hours go," he assures her. "Don't worry, I won't desert you."

William sits on his bed and stares at the veins on the back of his hands, the black and silver watch strapped onto his wrist.

Finally, Bree's fever's broken; she's feeling better. She's eating again. And her long day and night of suffering have come to an end with the best results, at least for now. *Thank God, thank you God.* These words from a lowly agnostic, a lousy ex-Jew, but please accept.

He and Claire, they've also lost days in the caretaking. Maybe it was only luck that saved him from booking a non-refundable ticket home as he was destined to miss that flight. Or maybe he's learned to proceed cautiously, to always consider worst-case scenarios before seeking out that best option.

But wow, this watch on his wrist does have power. It's always there to remind him of the time he's lost, hours and days spent nursing Bree that are no longer his to claim.

Still, he won't complain. He can only be glad he'd been so wrong about Claire. At five a.m. Tuesday, she'd taken Bree's temperature then waited to see if the fever climbed before waking him with a call. When he got to their room, she updated him: the fever was holding at 101°. As he'd checked labels on the pill containers Claire handed over, he noticed how her lips were so pale, how she seemed to be realizing cancer's not the flu, surprise.

He'd wondered in that moment if Bree's grand experiment had failed, his sister-in-law was done, but she'd surprised him, maybe herself too. Her pallor seemed to belie her willingness to keep going; she had taken notes on Bree's restless night, recorded every one of her requests. She'd laid down wet cloths and even remembered to feed her ice chips, the most his wife could stomach when it got that bad.

William had struggled for hours to figure out what level of sick they were dealing with beyond these masking drugs, but finally they'd agreed it was mostly a fever. They decided to keep Bree at the hotel if they possibly could, monitoring her in shifts to make sure she kept hydrated.

They tagged each other when clocking in, made bad jokes about the Ovarian Olympics and this marathon run.

When Bree's fever finally broke the next day, he'd lay his hand on her brow and reveled in the glorious gift of human sweat. Some ten minutes later, Claire came in with meals from McDonald's and he told her to get some sleep, adding how much she had impressed him with her nursing abilities, how lucky they both were to have had her near.

Claire seemed to tear up with the unexpected and probably rare compliment, or maybe it was simply exhaustion kicking in. The two shared a sausage breakfast with plastic forks, plastic everything as Bree slept; then impulsively, William hugged his sister-in-law. Their embrace was surprisingly intimate, wrapped in smells of rubbing alcohol and greasy meat, a sticky something laid on the back of his neck where her hand briefly touched, and the two of them inhabiting that nameless grey and always confusing space of man, woman, family.

Now only hours later he finds himself alone again, eyeing a view of black tar roofs, but also townhouses painted in flowerpot colors. The emergency's over and even if it wasn't, he knows Bree will be cared for. So should he stay in Charleston or should he leave?

The joke of his profession is that he understands why she doesn't want him here. *Bree doesn't want his weight. For all it may hurt then: don't be weight.*

But can he do what she asks?

"*I don't want you! Go away! Go back—.*"
"*Bree. Where, hon?*"
"*Go where you were before! Stay at the door!*"

178

Of course, he will, even if he doesn't always understand why. But he can't deny how he feels when he catches her looking his way as if he's no longer her husband, but some fearful stranger approaching her bed.

I'll take the damn hinges off! Then, you'll have to let me in!

And what was that? William grabs a breath. Perhaps it's not surprising he's tapped into so much anger rising from within. But what would any of his patients, colleagues, think if they knew these eruptions were coming so often and unexpectedly? They'd think the psychologist has lost his mind.

Yet these words—hadn't he heard them before? From someone who didn't seem at all concerned with the fallout or showing restraint?

It takes a moment or two for William to refocus, then... It had been a woman, the mother of a patient—Cal. Cal who? Cal Stepen. Yes, the boy had been a direct target of her threats, hinges off the door, and William a witness to their fierce battles.

Cal Stepen.

William moves to the desk and turns on his laptop to link into his office remotely, pull up the boy's file.

That witch of a mother had cut off Cal's visits before they'd made much progress, he remembers. Not that he ever had much hope for the kid. She'd routinely locked him in his room for prolonged periods of confinement. There wasn't a father to step in to referee and William himself had proved a poor surrogate.

So yeah, he's feeling like a failure recalling details of the case. But there has to be another reason he's also scrolling frantically to bring up Cal's file, read it through...

179

…Questions to indirectly explore with patient in future sessions: did his father act in ways that encouraged communications between mother and son? Or did the father put pressure on their already tenuous relationship, given his own alcoholism and presumed stresses in the marriage? What role did the father play in the family's stability and/or dysfunction when he was alive? And how will the two survivors fill the holes left by his absence; will they find or lose each other tending those holes?

William reads the last sentence two, three times.

The words themselves are a sinkhole of letters threatening to drag him in; push him under.

But here it is. The sentence William needs to understand most of all.

And how will the two survivors fill the holes left by his absence; will they find or lose each other tending those holes?

This last sentence so vague, overwritten even, not his usual style; he can't remember why his thoughts might have detoured into such murky depths. These other words were odd too. Why had he called Cal and his mother, survivors? That wasn't an objective description, not even close. Maybe he suspected they had survived something, but his notes that day showed he hadn't gathered enough evidence to support such conclusions.

And now that he's unearthed the lines, it's also clear he has no interest in the fate of the Stepen family. He might try to resume sessions with the boy when he returns to New York. But meanwhile here they are, he's summoned this family to Charleston, and why?

180

Will they find or lose each other tending those holes?

Is William the person who cannot find his loved ones? Draw them near?

Perhaps. Somehow he has become the person whose role has changed in Charleston, in his marriage, and no one's noticed the shift, not even him.

Now he stumbles into those ever-changing spaces only Bree can see and where he has no map, no compass, no abilities to communicate or repair.

Or is he a survivor?

No, he is the opposite of that, a threat to her, a trespasser. He intrudes in these rooms, hallways, but Claire was invited. He doesn't fit in this new space the Overton girls have laid down between them. Other Overtons not named, or perhaps never known to him, dwell there instead. They've had squatter rights for years.

And Bree wants it to be like that, with Claire down here and all of them here tearing fiercely, lovingly, obsessively, helplessly, at those decades-old family memories that dog her at every turn. He has no purpose or right to come in and upend.

So tread lightly. Take care not to disturb the others Bree wants near.

Let them move in while you move out.

Do not disturb any of them.

Go!

~30~

Back when Bree was first learning all the ways not only cancer but chemo could tear up a body, William was always finding her in the bathroom bent over porcelain and heaving up chunks of chalk-white, sometimes brown. Once, when she tried to clean up afterwards, she accidentally smacked her electric toothbrush on the wall with such force that one of the sconces shuddered and broke.

So no, she doesn't expect to find William in this same place, the door to the bathroom opened wide. But why wouldn't he? Thinking he was alone, he wouldn't have bothered with any locks. Still, he'd given her one of his keycards last week, asked her to visit, and now she was here feeling better, wanting to thank him for everything. She came looking for her husband, lover, but has walked in on an eleven-year-old boy. His pants are pushed down past his knees, and one of his hands is moving with such fast, frenzied motions below, she can only imagine that part of his body would surely plead for mercy if it could.

The expression on William's face as he reaches for what she can no longer give him is so pitiful and his breath comes in such spurts, like a biker who has traveled miles with no water. He is leaning over the toilet for balance, his other palm pressing against the wall. Maybe it is the fact he hunches to grab there, that he's not standing tall. But she doesn't say "Sorry," then close the door as she normally would to give him his privacy.

Instead, she clutches the doorknob and watches her husband finish himself off, his hand and ass shaking so hard. She is mesmerized by how only a little bit of cum spews out at the end; that it is always so small an act, after all.

No wonder he's needed her for all these years to make it so much more.

"I could've," she offers when he comes out, wiping his hands on a towel. But he shakes his head no, shuts that down.

"Okay. Then I came to tell you I'm feeling better."

She watches him pull clean slacks off a closet hanger, unbuckle his belt.

"I know Bree. I've been keeping tabs," he replies as he steps out, steps in.

"You've done more than that. Claire told me you saved us. You talked her through every step in the nursing, got me drugs that finally did the job. Not that I'm surprised," she says, trying to lighten the mood, "but you should know your sister-in-law's mighty impressed."

When he grimaces, she tries again.

"So anyway, I came to apologize."

"For what?"

"According to Claire, I said some horrible things to you."

"You didn't say anything. It just turned out I could help most as a go-between with Sands and the pharmacy this time. It was fine I stayed away."

Bree sighs. "I'm not saying I'm sorry Claire took over and you felt rejected. Are we talking about the same thing?"

"You tell me. You keep saying you need to get away from the old cancer routines. I'm part of all that. I get it. Meanwhile, Claire's gone through the last few days like a pro. We've got Sands paying attention to your case like he never has before. Where do I even fit in?"

"What are you saying now?" she ventures, hardly daring to believe he's standing before her, agreeing with all her old arguments.

Rather than replying, William rubs his forehead and frowns. His silence makes her even more nervous; she has to move about and absently picks up his watch lying on the desk. Cupping its shining face in her hands, she says, "What we've got to do is stop the calendar. You've been talking too much about getting me home for Christmas. Claire too. I don't like that you're both ganging up on me."

"Bree,"

"This year, the holidays will make everyone crazy whether I'm home for them or not," she insists.

"Did you hear what I said before?"

"I heard. And if you're saying you going to leave, yes, that makes me happy but not for the reasons you think. I'll be relieved, that's all. Do you want to know why?"

She lays the watch back on the table, grabs his hand.

"If you go home first, I'll be the one who has to miss you. Which I will, and which is something we hardly talk about anymore. How I can't bear it when *you're* not around."

His palms feel rougher than she usually remembers. Then again, they've been subjected to so many tedious duties since her cancer's return and toilet brushing, cooking, will bring up the calluses, they will.

She lets her finger trail one bluish vein until she reaches a spot where the skin pales. William normally straps his watch on this part of his wrist and yes, here's his marker, this lightened patch that confirms a daily routine.

But how many times has she looked this way barely registering its purpose except as a resting place for *her* eyes, *her* lips, *her* appreciation? As if even William's skin isn't simply his to clean and claim, but theirs?

"I will so miss you," she breathes.

~31~

"No games this time," he stipulates. "Will you trust me?"

She will. She has set up a time for them to meet while Claire's sunbathing poolside.

As he eases onto the couch, Bree's glance is foxlike, alert, and he's encouraged.

"Sands says your new meds will probably help you feel better right away," he tells her and then, as if trying to convince himself this is information that's relevant, *he's still relevant*, he passes her his notes. "Also, he wants you to consult with an oncologist he knows down here. Look, I wrote everything out for you and if you do these things regularly, I'll do what you want in return. I'll pack my bags and head home."

The lines around her lips go soft.

"I mean it. You've been saying that's what you want, so fine."

Oddly, Bree shakes her head as if she's refusing this blame. Then she asks, "It's not because of what happened in your room?"

"No! Don't be silly; we're married how long? I was only missing you."

But he senses he's sounding a little too vehement in his denial and steers the conversation back to Bree.

"Since we're being honest though, I do want to tell you something," he begins, grabbing a breath. "You've said

186

you've had these memories you can't let go of, they shake you to your core."

Bree starts to shake her head, no. "That's fever delirium, you can't make too much out of that."

"I'm not talking about the last few days. I'm saying for weeks now…Remember that day I walked in on you and you were lying on the bathroom floor, crying? When I asked what happened, all you could say was, 'It's not me being sick, it's not me being sick, I don't need you for this.'"

She doesn't say anything, but her nostrils flare ever so slightly, and he knows he's on the right track.

"Then later, you said something upset you, you couldn't even remember what. Look, I've been watching, this happens a lot Bree. But I don't know if you're having these feelings because of the pills you're taking? Or you're scared, or exhausted."

"It could be any of that," she says in a small voice, sounding more like a child than his wife.

"Or complications, or whatever. Not knowing, though, I can't call up Sands and ask him what to do next. So, I think we have to go another way. Maybe find you a specialist who's not all about the cancer but who's really good on this other stuff—."

"What kind of complications?"

'It's complex PTSD,' William thinks but doesn't say out loud. He's not ready to say more yet, not being sure of his facts, and not too knowledgeable on the disorder itself, if only because complex PTSD doesn't yet warrant its own listing in the DSM, the professional's bible of mental disorders.

Still, he has worked with patients suffering from acute PTSD over the years; from them, he's learned how some people can be so traumatized in the aftermath of a life-threatening event their memories can consume them, threatening their marriages, friendships, careers.

So, what would a diagnosis of complex PTSD mean they were up against? Everything, anything; often, a person suffering from complex PTSD has experienced multiple and repeated traumas for years.

Bree is waiting patiently for his explanation, finally engaged, and he feels badly about that. If she's so interested, her suffering might even be worse than he's suspected. Nonetheless, he certainly isn't willing to scare her off with his own show of nerves.

Instead he says, "We're talking about an anxiety disorder, that's all. If I go home now, I can vet some doctors before the holidays. I'll ask around, and when you're ready to come home—."

"Oh that's it," she sniffs, sounding relieved. "This is all your latest ploy to get me home."

He's caught off guard by her cynicism; *this isn't Bree.* Then again, what does he really know of this woman he's been dealing with in Charleston? Far less than he would've have believed he understood about his wife only weeks ago.

"We'll get you home on your terms," he replies, maintaining an even tone. "Besides, was this ever a permanent move? Is there something I'm missing?"

"No," she says meeting his gaze, and he's encouraged to go on.

"If you agree to follow Sands' instructions, I'll go. And maybe in three, four, weeks, I'll fly back—just to check on you."

"Huh. Three weeks."

"That's just after New Year's. Of course, you can come home earlier if you want. It's your choice."

"Claire and I haven't talked about where she'll be for the holidays," Bree murmurs. William observes his wife's confusion as she starts to realize this flight of hers might be reaching its end. How, yes, this has only been a migration and their next moves must bring them all home.

"I don't know how I feel about Christmas this year," she says then. "I mean I don't want to go back if our grandchildren are going to have to deal with something horrible, like me stuck in bed the whole time."

Like her mother, for nearly two years.

"No one's expecting anything Bree. If we go home but don't see the kids, they'll cope. Meanwhile, I'm ready to leave Charleston and start putting this new plan of ours in place. First, I'm going to find you a therapist. And while you're down here, I'll expect you to follow Sands' instructions to the letter.

"So can we agree or do we still have problems understanding each other? Tell me Bree. What do you want me to do?"

189

~32~

"We may be in for a bit of turbulence so I'd ask everyone to please return to their seats," the pilot announces over the speakers. William's not worried. He's been belted in the entire trip. He checks his wallet and considers whether he has time to buy himself a third Bloody Mary. These tiny vodka bottles can't really get the job done when the goal is to get trashed, blotto everything.

"Sir, will you push up your seat please? Sir?"

"I'm sorry?"

"Also, if you could just move your foot. The aisle needs to be clear."

She isn't pretty enough to be this bossy, he thinks, even while some part of him knows he's acting as peevishly as any child.

"I thought I said—," the attendant mutters, kicking the side of his seat with her shoe.

"Oh sorry."

"Thank you."

This time he nods amenably, but who cares? He is not nearly drunk enough and soon they are going to land. So sit back, William. Stop fighting all these losing battles and face all your new realities.

Starting with the most obvious: even with Claire as her roommate, Bree's clearly feeling alone in Charleston. That makes sense; this is what goddamn cancer has done to her the second time around. Now she's fighting two wars simultaneously, from within and without, like any soldier. She's facing physical and also emotional battles, but how much strength does she have left to take any of it on?

Because complex PTSD is serious stuff. He's learned a traumatized patient's mind can be both her merciless torturer and best ally. If certain memories threaten to overwhelm, the subconscious mind will bury them away so they're effectively forgotten, sometimes for years.

So then the therapist has to go further. He has to listen for disconnects, be on guard for false narratives.

And he has to raise up the near-dead from their memories, and pulse-rocking terrors, lift up shrouds and make them cradles while he urges his patient to close her eyes and buy into the lullaby he's pushing, *"It was near-death, but you're here. It was near-death, but there's no such thing, only life over here. Only life and who's going to convince me life is near-death or far from one moment to the next, no one can, because there's no logic in that, find the logic, I dare you!"*

The plane shudders off a wind, rouses William from his half-doze. Everything he's been studying about complex PTSD has played out in Bree's behavior over the few months. She left New York in a panic. Then she'd summoned Claire to Charleston as if she had an urgent need to connect up with her and revisit their shared pasts. Yet she couldn't have explained her motives to anyone if asked. She didn't understand them herself.

William guesses he can take some blame too. Probably he shouldn't have pushed her away when she'd first asked him to counsel her; he would've done a lousy job, yes, but not for the reasons he believed at the time. And maybe he shouldn't have left Charleston until he'd lined up a therapist in that city who specialized in complex PTSD.

191

But he hadn't done that work deliberately, childishly, selfishly; fearing if she was able to find her supports in that southern city, she'd have her best argument for not returning home.

Also, he should've clued Claire into Bree's unfinished business. After all she'd done for them, the least she deserved was a heads-up on trouble.

But doctor. How can you be expected to help her with any of this—when you're no longer allowed to care?

"Looks like we're in luck folks, we dodged a tailwind," the pilot tells his passengers. Good job, William silently cheers. For aren't pilots a bit like therapists? Both perform in similar ways—William has to continually monitor changes in a patient's behavior just as a pilot must constantly check his gauges to adjust for shifts in altitude and velocity. Both he and the pilot must be responsible for strangers who trust them with their lives. And to deliver their best in any consistent way, they must see their jobs not as a series of disconnected tasks but rather as a marathon they are always training for. They must pace themselves because slow and steady is a winning strategy; strive for a healthy balance of proper nutrition, rest, exercise…

His old running regimen demanded these same rhythms, he realizes. His running then; his clinical work now; tending to Bree…All these challenges demand the same skill sets, didn't they? A willingness to bear up under trials: to endure. You learn to absorb the hard smacks on pavement until one day the jolt's gone and you can focus on what's straight ahead. You can move towards that goal with confidence. Don't look down though, or you'll stumble for sure.

No, you're drunk. You're an ass.

The stumble is all William can focus on now.

The plane hits the ground with the smallest of bumps; it's not anything to remark on and then it's gone. No one else is reacting as if this landing's unusual in any way. They're clicking off their seatbelts before the safety lights are turned off; they're pulling down their bags from the overheads.

William's in no rush to join them so he hangs back in his seat. Without Bree, he doesn't feel any sense of urgency and besides he's had all that bad liquor, how many Marys?

Against his closed eyelids, he feels a drumming. Maybe he's drunk, maybe he's not. But he senses an inner prod and, in a moment of clarity, suspects these urgent feelings may not be tied to Bree.

Perhaps he simply wants to find his balance again, all those old rhythms. The pilot has dropped the plane's wheels onto the tarmac with perfect timing, and you need to be just as steady, William. Steady as she goes. You need to get your mind and body in sync. That's how you'll regain control of your life no matter what choices Bree makes for herself. And that's how you'll hold on for the marathon, survive every treacherous turn.

Just hold on.

~33~

Bree had been looking forward to a Charleston fish fry breakfast, but Claire slept stubbornly through their wake-up call. When her sister awakes, she decides to order up room service as her apology, an Asian meal for two. In yet another surprise, she pulls out a present for Bree from her luggage, teal Chinese slippers embroidered with tiny pink roses. The gift might have been altogether charming except for the fact the slippers were still wrapped in clear plastic packaging tagged with a price sticker, $4.99.

Claire slips on her own pair of new slippers so they can lounge then flips through the room service menu. She starts to read their options aloud but halfway through, launches into a story of how her latest boyfriend hates Asian food.

"Oh Bree, you know Asian's my favorite, it's always been," she says, picking up the house phone to dial in their order. "I mean back when we were kids when—hello? Yes. I'd like to place an order for the Jianbing made with tuna. The tuna."

Bree knows the spiciness of certain dishes combined with her meds might not sit well, so maybe Chinese is not her best choice. Nonetheless, soon dishes are delivered to their room along with forks and chopsticks. As they eat, Claire's in a fine mood; she tells another tale Bree hasn't heard before.

"I played this game when I lived in the city, did you know? I lived just a subway stop over from Chinatown so why not? I'd call up my friends, and I'd tell them, 'Hey so and so, congratulations. You just won the Chinese lottery.'" Her fingers stained with cocktail sauce sweep the air to entice her audience of one. "'Drop what you're doing and let's go out, I'll buy you dinner. But hey, also, this is your one-time only invite. You know Dustin Hoffman in that movie, *Kramer vs. Kramer*? When he wanted that job at the holiday party, but no one was ready to give him the time of day? He said, now or never, make your choice, and he got the job just on his rooster strutting, you know? That's how it is with my Chinese lottery, friend. Here's food, a free dinner, and hey I like you, but it's now or never. If you say no tonight, you're at the bottom of my list again; you won't be called for a very long time.'"

Claire moves about the salt and pepper shakers sitting on the kitchen table, still laughing at her own bullying tactics from years past. She sits the pepper atop the salt and for just a moment, balances one perfectly on the other. Clapping her hands in glee, she sidles a look at her sister as if waiting for her to join in, and though she's met with silence, she seems to take no offense.

"Is this food making you sleepy, by the way?" she asks her, still smiling in unabashed triumph, "Did we forget to ask them to take out the MSG?"

"No, I reminded you," Bree replies. "I know the drills by heart."

"Good." But just as her sister's relaxing in her chair, her ringtone goes off, Santana's "Black Magic Woman." Claire clicks off her cell, not bothering to check the caller ID, but Bree notices she nonetheless appears irritated.

She can only guess who might be trying to reach her back home.

"Aren't you going to answer that?"

Claire shakes her head in fierce refusal. "I want an hour away from the drama. I'm enjoying having nothing to worry about except our dessert."

"Still you should call," Bree urges. "If it's Daniela, something could be wrong."

Claire frowns. "It's gonna be her."

Exaggerating every move, she leans over and checks the screen. "Uh huh, it is."

She sweeps a bit of unruly hair off her face but after a few moments, abruptly rises from her chair and leaves Bree, as if needing to find her privacy in some other part of the suite. As she departs, her slippers make soft shuffling sounds on the tiles.

Bree tries to get down a few more forkfuls as Claire makes her call, although a migraine is starting to ribbon either side of her head. While she is not trying to eavesdrop, she can hear her sister's voice coming up hard against the wall, demanding, "What is it?" Then,

"Damn it, Daniela! So you've already done it? What does the doctor say? Well, how bad? Yes, you should've called, don't give me that! But your dad says he's on his way? He knows where you are?"

Eager to make some noise that might cut out the rest, Bree moves to the counter with dirty plates, hers and Claire's. She's ready to scrape then head to the bedroom to gather up sheets for the maids. But suddenly she feels a swell of memory rising up from some unknown place inside, an angry tide,

"No. Now sit down, shut up."

And their mother is giving Claire her medicine, bringing on the screams. Claire begs her, "Mama no!" She's dying; it tastes so bad. Only when she starts gagging, does their mother turn to Bree. "Now get your father, go get him."

Dad.

Dad.

"Go get your father! Now Bree!"

Her sister is screaming so hard.

But no now sit down shut up, and Bree is confused. She always runs as fast as she can to bring Dad back home. She knows the front door of that house is always open and so she doesn't stop doesn't dawdle but heads straight for the pink kitchen where she knows Dad always drinks his coffee with the lady next door. She cries, "Come back home, Claire's sick again! Please, please!"

"I'm serious, you're not going to hold me hostage from across the country. Handle your own crap! You're not going to win, Daniela! What I'm doing here with your aunt I can't walk away from and now you pull this? You deal with your father then, make him handle it!"

"Asshole!" Bree hears her sister curse, but their fight's too hard to follow, too cruel on Claire's part, and her insides start to ache. Is it normal to want to protect a niece she hardly knows from her mother's swift anger? *Tell me now, now, or you're back at the bottom of my list!*

At some point, the call ends and Claire returns to the kitchen. Her sister's cheeks appear flushed, but otherwise she doesn't give off any sign of being disturbed by this most recent battle with Daniela. She glances at Bree as if bothered more by the sight of her sick sister cleaning plates and volunteers, "Well, she went ahead and got a belly piercing. Now she's sitting around the house to see if there's any pus or blood since her friends said to keep an eye out for infections. Can you believe this?"

Like a reel on a rod dragging Bree in, *can you believe?*

"The good news is Trevor's heading out to be with her. I tell you that man was an ass with me, but he always shows up when it comes to the kids."

Bree nods. She's feeling aches in her groin, one snaking spasm starting to circle another, and she's having trouble understanding all her sister needs to share. She does hear Claire say something about Trevor and Daniela, all these people she loves but can no longer count on for her happiness. And she feels for Claire who has these new worries, all these problems they couldn't have imagined only an hour ago.

Pushing off another stab of pain, she manages, "Are we finished with Charleston then?"

199

This unexpected query seems to throw Claire. She doesn't answer right away, but instead walks over to the window and pulls the drape cord.

"I don't think so," she finally says. "Unless we get a call from Trevor, there's no emergency. No, let's have a good day, forget New York."

She turns her gaze to the street below.

"It's starting to rain but that shouldn't stop us," she says.

Dad, I need your dad. Go get your dad, Bree. Go over to her house and get him now! Tell him Claire's sick, so come, come come!

Bree corrals a breath as Dr. Sands has taught her and the physical pain—unlike this other anguish she's feeling—unhinges for the moment.

"Claire, I think you should go. If your girls need you, it's selfish for me to keep you here."

Her sister makes a whistling noise through her nose.

"Bree, I don't want to fight you too, but you should stay out of this, okay? Trust me. Home's not where I'm needed most."

She eyes Bree as if she is willing to go further if challenged. And yes, Bree is ready to let it go, but then suddenly the pain from *that* day is on her again, riding up her throat and also coming up from below.

"But you're her mother!" she cries.

There's a long warming silence as everything rolls. Claire seems to be squinting to gauge her sister's new show of authority before she retorts, "Oh you're the best at mothering, everyone says! So you'd know!"

"If you don't go then I have to," Bree hears herself reply.

"What does that mean?" her sister demands.

But Bree is already moving from the kitchen into the hall. She's hurrying, but she does remember to pick up her cellphone and keycard off the side table near the door. *I might need these.* She's grateful for this one clean thought slicing through all that pain. She understands she has to move fast, find air, or she won't have a chance.

"Wait. I'm sorry for what I said, Bree," she can hear as she reaches the door.

But didn't Claire say something about rain, how it was raining outside?

She heads out to the hall.

   Someone is holding the elevator for her.

      Lucky.

Only after reaching the street, does Bree realize Claire's wrong; a few puddles glisten on the pavement but any shower has passed. Still, she's glad for the damp air as she usually has an easier time catching her breath in this kind of weather. Or so she tells herself.

Then she steps off the curb and pain saddles her again.

These spasms don't move out from the usual places where her coiled snakes hide; this time, they're up in her chest, her arms. She knows the stabs in the groin are tied to her cancer's advance, but these aren't the same. Maybe this new weighted drag she's feeling in her arms is nothing but dread, though…thoughts pushing up like a stubborn weed's bloom...

She tries walking faster, but can't get this pain to pour down her legs or out onto the sidewalk widening every crack…she's not surprised. These snaking weeds will continue to grow wild, if ignored…and that's the trick… once she notices them, they can no longer surprise…

"Bree, sit down! I'm watching your sister, that's my job not yours. You wait until I tell you to get your dad. Not yet, it's not that bad yet."

Their mother turns back to Claire; she's more than ready to step in at the first sign of trouble even if the child's still laughing, clapping at Bree's dizzying twirl that sends her from one end of the kitchen to the other. Her little sister may be smiling but that doesn't change the fact she's sick and don't be fooled.

So as Bree watches, she gives Claire another squirt of something brown and fishy-smelling from the dropper, and another. Until her sister starts to whimper, shake; brown wet starts to drip down each leg. Until she starts to hold her stomach and scream such a scream, Bree hardly notices when her mother gives up and half-drags her sister to the bed, not the bathroom but bed. And she can't think fast enough when her mother comes back to the kitchen, demanding, "Now! Now it's time Bree. So go, run. Your dad's at her house, let him know Claire's sick! She's sick again, so tell him to come!"

And no, Aunt Syl's not sick. Not even Mom was sick when Bree was eight and knew how to twirl. Only Claire had been sick then: Claire.

In all those years no one viewed any of the youngest sister's complaints as serious, no one ever tended to Baby's make-believe. Not Eileen and no, not Bree either. But why not?

Simply this: none of them could remember all they had each gone and buried deep, deep, inside those days.

Shaking, she pulls out her cell. She has to call Sophie. She's a lawyer who knows what to do when secrets are buried deep.

Shut up, sit down, Bree. Shut up, no one's sick now Bree, but you, you, and so what can you believe? You can't. The side effects of self-medicating are confusing you...

When Sophie answers the phone, Bree can hear her surprise, "Mom, how are you? Is everything okay? Are you coming back soon?"

"No, Sophie." But what else does she want to tell her now that they're talking?

"You're not coming home yet?"

"I'm not ready," she breathes out. "Soon."

Sophie's voice hardens in response. "Okay, that's fine."

"Sophie, listen to me."

"Just tell me this, Mom. Are you going to see a doctor down there?"

"I don't want to talk about that either."

Bree looks down as if what she does want to say can somehow be found on the street and notices she is still wearing those silly Chinese slippers. She'd left the hotel and in her rush, hadn't thought to change. What a strange sight she must be; more oddly, why hasn't this sidewalk startled her up from her mistake with all its sharp-edged bumps and grooves?

And what does she want, no, need to tell Sophie?

Bree, you don't know anything about this so sit there and be quiet! Let me think for a minute!

"Your Aunt Claire."

"Aunt Claire? What about her?"

She closes her eyes, tries to focus. "Your aunt, she's been staying with me. She told me—I haven't been fair with you. She thinks we should be talking whenever my condition changes in any big way. So about a week ago, I did have, um, a fever. Your father was down here, he knows all about it."

206

But Bree is vaguely worried she's detouring away from the real news she needs to share. Other confessions have to be made, especially those only her daughter deserves to hear.

"Also Aunt Claire said, well, the odds are starting to look lousy for all the girls in our family when it comes to my type of cancer. You can't guess how sorry I am about that, but I'm not sure she's right. Just because I have cancer doesn't mean you will."

"Mom?"

"All I wanted was to keep you safe and now! That's the, the,"

"Mom!"

Hearing that word again, "Mom!" Bree realizes she didn't call Sophie to share this news either. No, she wants to talk about *her* mother, all she's starting to suspect that woman did to her daughters when no one else was around. Like too many droppers of sick, enough to bring their dad back home whenever he stayed too long at Therese Rupin's. Sophie defends minors in court; maybe she can help.

But Bree has so much to explain she's afraid she won't be able to slow down her thoughts, tell her all she needs to say. Besides, her daughter's voice is tugging her in the wrong direction.

Suddenly, she feels a great need to hide and looks about. She finds shade under a store awning where handbags are sold. In the window, a black and pink polka-dot scarf slides out of a faux crocodile purse like a smoothly gliding creature at the aquarium, showing all its teeth.

And in that same window's reflection, Bree sees herself as others would, a sick ostrich wearing brown capris and a yellow striped shirt. Feathered grey hairs peek out from under the blonde; the whole trembles lightly off a breeze. She doesn't have makeup on, she realizes. She'd left so quickly.

Still staring at her mirrored self she cradles the phone and whispers to Sophie as if her daughter's right by her side, "I'm sorry." She wants to say she would speak more loudly except she can't. Damp air's needed or she'll lose her breath altogether.

Instead, she starts talking as fast as she can, trying to share with her daughter everything she knows before the pain and fear completely take over. She tells Sophie how much trouble she is facing against this reflection. What's been simmering inside for years.

"Mom?"

And now her daughter's talking and her voice is softer, coddling Bree as if *she* was the child. "Mom. Promise me, you'll hang up and go find Aunt Claire. Are you listening?"

Bree doesn't have an answer. She leans against the window and finds a spot where the flat glass pane offers cool relief, but little protection. She realizes she'd also left the hotel without a hat. In this dampness, wearing these slippers, the bumpy sidewalk is coming up through her soles...

"Mom," Sophie is asking, "Will you hang up and head back to the hotel?"

"I will," she promises before saying her goodbyes, and certainly she means to.

Still when she clicks off, she stares at the blank faceplate with a kind of wonder. She must have meant to call Sophie, because she took her phone and hotel keycard with her when she left the hotel. But not a hat or wallet, not cash. And again, why these slippers?

Suddenly, someone touches her shoulder. Bree turns to see a balding man wearing tinted sunglasses. The glasses make him seem unfriendly, although his smile is kind.

"Are you all right, ma'am?" he asks, in a southern drawl that makes each word sound as if it's dangling from a string.

When he asks her if she needs a ride home, she can see his blue Chevy van in plain sight, parked at the curb. Its door on the passenger side is already swung wide waiting for someone, maybe for her. She feels badly when she says "no," in a way that implies he's not a good Samaritan, but instead a man who preys on women who are perhaps slightly drunk or tired at the wrong hour of the day. She must've insulted him for he then seems eager to simply get in the van and drive away.

Still, Bree's relieved when he leaves. She doesn't have the strength to explain herself to anyone else today.

And that means she should probably move away from this handbag store before the owner calls the police. She guesses the hotel is two, maybe three, blocks away. If Bree can just pull herself together, she should have no problem heading back. Hadn't Sophie suggested the same thing just moments ago?

Besides, Claire is at the hotel waiting for her. She has to take care of Claire.

As she looks again at her feet, tries to reorient herself to the general direction of the hotel, she notices how minute bits of quartz have been expertly laid into the cement below. Maybe they're quartz, maybe crystal. Or maybe they're pieces of candy, Hansel and Gretel.

209

She's too tired to stoop down and find out what's
digging into the soles of her slippers, candy or rocks. But
she could probably gather up these shards if she wasn't so
tired or her capris had pockets, if all these pebbled dogs'
eyes didn't wink and then shimmer away as she drew near.

Or she could pick up some to bring back to Claire,
but then what? What more would they then be forced to
understand, what news to share, as they move through the
rest of this day?

~34~

As the only child in an Orthodox Jewish home, he'd been raised on so many stories. His favorite? The story of Joseph rising to power after he correctly interpreted Pharaoh's dreams. Prepare for years of fatted cows; and also years where the herds lay down to die. Be not content with seven years of plenty. *Prepare for the years of drought.*

Or Leviticus: lay aside a portion of your fields for the poor to gather for their tables when no one is watching. Don't be greedy and harvest only for yourself. And never make a man, woman, or child feel shame simply because you looked their way. Also, leave each field fallow in its seventh year so the land can replenish itself: test your patience with every season.

But what is a farmer thinking when he relinquishes fertile ground? What can he possibly feel as he prepares to give over his field to God for a year, knowing he only owns the one? Will he then have to scavenge when dusk falls; fill his stomach off the corners of a neighbor's yield? And how long can he live believing faith will carry him through, with no other promises, no guarantee?

That farmer would have to cast his eye over a barren landscape and for the sake of God, restrain.

For the sake of a future you can neither conjure nor imagine: restrain.

For the sake of a bird's ability to find a fat worm in this soil next spring: restrain.

Dreams of restraint were couched in William's upbringing. Yet from these injunctions of formal religion, William has absolutely turned.

Science helped him more. This Science made no demands on the soul or begged its restraint. These days, we can use scientific tools to understand otherwise terrifying behaviors of Nature, humans too. We can calculate parts to the whole and know exactly how much to cut away, or cure. We can learn how to stay safe, prosper by preparing.

But now Science isn't working for him either. Science and all its formulas are finally abandoning William and Bree.

To quell his anguish, he has become a bit desperate in a search for something else. Religion, booze, even pillowcases that still hold her smell. Three sweet things and this last particularly visceral; what he wants in hand.

For William desires to have Bree not only close, but able to be swallowed whole. He needs to gorge on memories of her when she's away, ravage her when she's near. In almost a complete renunciation of his years of medical training, he finds himself frantic for what's no longer within his physical reach, his mental grasp, all he will never know.

They sit together, as always, wrapped in the familiar intimacies he has come to rely on in this office. Frank Paley's tie will crease at the point where he has laid the tie bar irregularly on an angle. The oversized terrarium on the sill will distract with an indistinct but flemmy smell. An antique Persian rug on the floor begs to be vacuumed but is too often ignored. And his mentor will wait for him to speak first, measuring the time in between sips of hot tea.

"Maybe I didn't appreciate her enough," William admits, loathing his whining tone but unable to stop. "I didn't convince her she was well-loved. That's why I'm being punished."

"Funny. You keep calling this separation a punishment."

"That's how it feels."

Frank Paley leans forward in his chair, tapping its worn edge.

"Sure. But you wouldn't describe what Bree's going through as a punishment, would you? I mean, she's suffering terribly. But punishment is a different word."

"I don't want to make this a semantics game, Frank. She doesn't deserve any hand she's been dealt. But if *I* add to her troubles with my worries, well, that's inexcusable, selfish, and yes, I should pay the price."

The clinician levels his gaze.

"Since her last diagnosis, you've both been forced to live with the question, 'What comes next?' Am I right? So don't fool yourself. You don't get to control any of this."

William swallows hard. He leans in to confide, "Frank, I know I'm guilty. Somewhere along the road, I failed her. Why else would she run? Who leaves home to die?"

"She told you she wants to be with her sister, so there's a clue," Paley argues. "You agreed they needed to iron out some family history before your wife can find some peace. It's not that she ran from you. No, she's seeking out something that has little to do with you."

"Listen Frank, I can't wait. I have to stay close because, well, I'm pretty sure Bree is struggling with PTSD."

Paley's glance narrows.

213

"Are you sure? It's not uncommon for people facing death to turn to their memories, good and bad. If she's sharing more than usual that's to be expected."

"That's not it," he insists, shaking his head. "I think maybe Bree was traumatized hearing her cancer had returned. Or perhaps she suffered PTSD during her first treatments, but no one knew with everything else she was going through. Either way, she's struggling with both cancer and trauma now. I think it's complex PTSD by the way. She seems to be dealing with so many memories that blindside but she doesn't want to share. With a cancer diagnosis, at least people understood and rallied round. Look, I don't know the specifics, and really I don't think Bree does either. But I've studied her as objectively as I can."

"You're explaining it well," Paley says, encouraging.

William pushes on, feeling the weight in each of his words, "She's still trying to deny she's suffering from both illnesses, but you sit with her and you can hear, see, the leaks."

Paley exhales and his breath smells like ginger, a Chinese ginger tea dragon with a long, coiling tail.

"Okay," he agrees. "Then we'll have to get her the right kind of help. I know people who specialize in this, and I can act as your go-between to set this up quickly. Also, we should contact her oncologist, bring him on board.

"And I'm going to write you a prescription, William. Nonrenewable but it'll help you sleep. We've got to give you some relief for the pain you're carrying around."

Frank smiles at him in that friendly, familiar manner, but then holds the moment a tick longer than usual. Waiting for him to get on with it please. And yes, this is a psychologist's job. They will give a patient permission to make his narratives bigger and more important than any clock moving to the hour's conclusion. But at the end of the session both client and therapist are expected to stand, maybe shake hands, and one will return to the waiting room feeling a bit shaky as he tries to sort through; the other is already thinking about his next appointment.

Today, William hardly knows how to respond. How can he begin to show his gratitude for the man's kindness? Should he express relief, joy? Or confess he feels a sense of calm coming on, teasing him with its promise that maybe, maybe, the PTSD can be stopped in its tracks. That someone might yet convince his wife there's time to take on this new foe, a victory can be had, and through clarity gained, insights made, she will find the peace she's looking for.

So what to say back? "Thank you." Then, "What's next?" And not, "Don't misunderstand, I'm not the patient here." No, rein in your ego, William, accept the prescription. Your mentor's not questioning your judgment as a psychologist or a husband. He's just offering an exhausted spouse the support he needs when the good fight's coming to an end. Don't be so proud you can't accept all these gifts coming your way.

And for the sake of this wife who's been caged for too long in prisons no one can see, let others come forward who can help her in ways you never could.

Step back and be grateful for all these strangers who will sit with her ghosts.

Step back and be grateful, William. Restrain.

~35~

Claire surveys every inch of her, every crease. She takes her hand so gently Bree knows she could pull away if she wants to, but she won't.

"Come in, Bree. I was worried about you. I went down to the street, but I couldn't find you," her sister confesses.

Bree can't follow much of what Claire's saying. Still, she can remember why she's returned to the suite.

"I think I owe you an apology."

"An apology for taking off? No, that's stupid."

"I wanted to figure things out alone, but I couldn't. Not completely."

Claire's mouth pinches up as if she can't hold back her frustration with everything that's already happened this morning. "Just don't—all right? Yeah, Daniela's call put a hitch in our plans, but nothing we can't reschedule. So, let's start this day again, figure it all out tomorrow. Okay?"

"Yes."

"Good. Great. Look at me, I need a tissue," her sister complains, holding up a palm stained with mascara. She heads for the bathroom, calling behind her, "You look tired Bree. How about a bath to relax in, we've got this great gorilla-sized tub. Big enough for the two of us, so just like the old days, huh?"

Bree blinks. She does feel tired. She heads into the bathroom where Claire is indeed standing over the oversized tub, her head cocked in invitation. It's modern, impressive, with six spa jets and beige marbled ribbing.

"A bath? Sure," she repeats, but then hears how slowly she's putting forward each word. To her own ears, she sounds drunk. But her sister has made herself busy at the tub and doesn't seem to notice. She is turning on the taps, cold and hot, a merge. Water starts up then cascades noisily onto the tub's ribbed bottom.

"Bubbles?" Claire invites, picking up a cherry-colored bottle and unscrewing the cap. "Let's go all out. What do you think?"

To all these suggestions Bree is quiet, compliant. It is hard to keep up, but at least her sister's talking softly as she helps Bree out of her striped shirt, undoing all those small buttons.

Bree's capris fall into a puddle on the floor and then Claire strips down. She has a younger body, perhaps, but also one that surprisingly shows more scars than the cancer patient. She doesn't say a word when Bree takes off the Chinese slippers with their shredded bottoms and throws them in the small gold wastebasket near the sink. She only reaches for her arm, helps her into the tub.

The water's high over the jets, or at least foaming bubbles give this impression. Bree makes herself comfortable against one grooved end of the tub. Then she closes one eye so Claire can only be viewed through the other.

And yes, she's grateful. The heat of the bath is such a different heat than on the street. Steam hits her in the face here too, but softly, as if someone is holding her chin up for kissing. She can feel her sister's toes as Claire moves to give them both more room. While this is a big tub, they still must adjust to fit.

They have certainly shared smaller spaces, the Overton girls. As children, they would sedate each other with soapy baths in a narrow but deep tub for hours; their eyes closing against the assault of bubbles, the other parts of their bodies more than willing to surrender to clumsy scrapings with the long brush. The brush would hunch them over and away from its barbed prongs as they passed it between them, washed each other's backs—even as the old basin's curved bottom took away their ability to shimmy away to safety when rough brush strokes came their way.

These memories rise up to comfort. Still, she wants to close her eyes against any bit of pain that might still surprise, or today's conversation with Sophie. Everything: everything.

Claire pulls a washcloth off a wall handle and runs it along her thigh. She's smiling but her eyes look black and squashed after too many arguments...

And all Bree can think is it's been Claire perched out on the ledges of dunking tanks her entire life. She has always seemed to be waiting, waiting for someone to hit the bull's eye, send her south. At any moment, there's going to be this smack, then all this water pulling her sister down to where she can't open her mouth but the water will come in, the words can't get out, and confessions can't be made or heard.

When the baptism's in a dunking tank, the water can get so filthy...

Bree takes a breath. If she dares to share any of the memories that toppled her this morning, how would that go? Would Claire also then remember?

Her sister's voice is low and muffled, beckoning her near. "You doing okay Bree?"

As she nods her response, she thinks, *'Whatever happens, then or now, Claire's survived. Yes, she has.'*

And what had her sister told her once before? In another hotel room—what had she said?

"Nothing exists. Carry on anyway."

So does her sister know?

Does she know?

Telling herself to calm down only stirs up her contrariness, and suddenly Bree pushes up on her knees to rise out of these warm suds. As she stands, she retrieves a drinking cup off the counter, *With Our Compliments*, printed in gold script on plastic.

"Claire. I want to take care of you for once," she announces. "Close your eyes."

Claire seems puzzled but obliges her and Bree tumbles a cup filled with water onto her scalp, to rinse. When she pours water on her sister's head a second time, to get out the bubbles, all she has been fighting inside falls away too.

Claire coughs on the next pour then protests, "Too much!"

"I'll be gentle," Bree assures.

She will be, of course. But then suddenly her left hand starts to shake; she can't keep this promise made.

Bree grabs a breath to ride it out—

And Claire is a girl dashing out of the bathroom while their mother stands over the toilet holding a jar filled with petroleum jelly and a fine-toothed comb. "You're not leaving this house Claire 'til we get every one!"

But Claire's found her hiding place by now; she's gone.

Finally, her mother gives up. She hands the job over to Bree and directs, "You do it when she comes back. My eyes are tired today."

And so Bree had, because no one else would.

"Remember your—lice? Claire?" she murmurs.

Claire blinks in surprise.

"Ugh. Don't make me. How much did you like pulling my hair so I cried?"

Not true. The lice picking had turned out to be Bree's special and unwelcome torture. Maybe she hadn't suffered the same fate as her sister, but she did lie in bed that night, terrified the lice had crept under her nails in the cleaning and would come to infect her too. No she hadn't loved those hours tending her sister's scalp with a magnifying glass and both of them locked in that bathroom, isolated from the rest of the family to keep them safe. But she didn't resent, either. This is what we do for each other, as sisters, what we've always done. We take care.

"That was some job," she does say. "Even Mom couldn't handle it."

Claire only seems repulsed by the memory. She makes a face so fierce Bree can't help but laugh, then she sneers, "Not couldn't, Bree. Wouldn't. I remember exactly what happened that day. So don't let Mom off with the usual excuses."

She takes the cup from Bree and pulls her sister back into the bath, making sure she settles into a tender sling of welcoming elbows and knees.

"Shush, let me," she says, as she starts to pour water onto her head. "Let me, please. I need you to understand. You didn't hurt me, big sister. No one else has ever cared for me as well."

As Bree lies back in Claire's arms, a cooling shudder passes through her.

Not couldn't. Wouldn't.

Not couldn't. Wouldn't.

Maybe, somehow, Claire has always known—in some place inside, sealed like a letter, or a vault. She knows and nothing more needs to be said. Bree can relax.

What Bree remembers, Claire remembers. They tie up together.

And this is what we do. We take care. We pick ourselves off the street and we take the bird home and we throw out our shredded shoes and we always watch out for each other because no one else will.

Even the wall mirror can no longer give back a reflection that isn't blurred under all this steam.

But it doesn't matter. She doesn't need to see herself cry. Salt is mixing with soap and Claire is propping her up between her raised knees so even where she wants to sink, she won't.

Since her last cancer diagnosis, she's been seeing her mother's face not only in her dreams, but also when she's awake. At first Bree wanted to believe Mary Overton had returned to save her daughter from a premature death, much as she'd once saved herself.

Here's the truth: that woman wouldn't save anybody. Not couldn't. Wouldn't. She never would.

And it's queer, isn't it? Bree once thought memories of her mother might protect her against all that threatened, so she'd let her in. Now Claire's telling her no, that trail leads nowhere, it never has. Those few years it all went on, Mom couldn't even bring their father home.

As she grooms her, Claire's fingers tangle in strands of Bree's blond-grey hair. Soon, her rinsing has skimmed her clean, clean down to the scalp…

And it all comes down to this. Underneath this world—where what we see we know and we tell—there's another. An entirely strange concoction built on dirt which cakes for too long on the heels, lodges under nails, rides up on hair. This other world has traveled with Bree for too many years. It's been a bad surprise to learn how long.

Still there's time…Claire has promised…for all that's crusted to rinse off in watery, wondering blasts…Then there can be an altogether new surprise…tied simply to surviving it all…

There's time. There's always been. Even if the Overton girls didn't get the love they needed before, there's still time. Surprise.

~36~

William rubs at the frosted glass, trying to view the damage outside. The snow is banking both front tires on the Lexus, and if he doesn't handle the overflow he'll be stuck with a tougher job shoveling the driveway later. Perhaps it might even become an impossible chore given this morning's injury; again, he curses this universe set against him.

It had been the snow blower stalling near Sophie's old swing set. They should have cleared that area years ago, but hadn't. So the wooden beam set on an uneven patch of dirt came into contact with the machine along the back walkway, its blades jammed, and his left hand had been torn up badly in the collision.

'Not a disaster,' he'd thought at first, but just to be safe he'd rushed inside the house to shove his bleeding knuckles under cold running water at the sink. Now he isn't so sure. Despite the rinsing, the back of his hand has puffed out from thumb to pinky finger to suggest the shape of a baby bird—and a throbbing has started up underneath, just like a baby bird's heart.

After a while (how long?) he turns the tap off, but then starts to feel both faint and cold. Most probably, his queasiness isn't tied to his physical injury at all, only stress, he reminds himself as any good psychologist would. Whatever the reasons, it makes sense to open up a bottle of gin and let the pained bird, fly, fly away. If drinking doesn't work, there'll be time to head to the hospital, deal with stitches later. But right now he doesn't want to think about a trip to the emergency room as part of this goddamned morning too.

'Here is true and complete failure,' he thinks as he then heads upstairs to rifle through the bathroom cabinets for wrapping gauze, aspirin. Drinking at ten thirty in the morning? Yes, he'd surely think any patient who told him that's how he got going in the a.m. pretty weak.

Still thanks to Bree's cancer, they had a great medicine chest. Besides her prescriptions, they had plenty of Pepto Bismol, diuretics, hemorrhoid creams. He periodically went into his stash first, then hers, for any number of remedies. His own need to be strong for Bree's sake often became his only rationalization for such obscene hauls.

His toes inch forward on the bathmat as he leans in to inspect today's lineup in the cabinet. Reptilian toes: he is a cold-blooded creature. He catches his foot and nearly stumbles, grabs the edge of the counter to be saved. And this is his new reality that can't be ignored; sober or sloshed, William is feeling fearfully out of balance in all ways.

Mindless chores like finding a toilet paper roll are probably all he can handle in his current state. From the recesses below the sink, he digs out a new four-pack hidden behind a soldierly lineup of disposable razor boxes, an Oil of Olay kit, Glade Strips. Bree always bought this stuff in bulk; he hasn't kept up the inventory.

But before he can make a mental note to sort through the lot, he is hugging himself by the shoulders and then, quick, it is all in the toilet. Just in time to spill out last night's dinner: lettuce, liquor. Then breakfast. Then all the bad meat and coins and goldfish ever consumed by anyone on a bet.

Shit. Oh, shit.

He smells an odor like bananas rotting, turns on the faucet. One miserable truth latches on when the stink doesn't pass: *he doesn't know how to fix pain when it comes.*

Beyond the mirror's reflection, William can see past the open door to their bedroom: the oversized armoire they share, their cluttered bookshelves, the clothes he wore yesterday tossed on the wingchair. This is the scene he will be facing every day if he chooses to simply ignore the mess. But why should he bother to straighten up? What part of this has any meaning for him now?

Oh, but what a pity party he is giving himself. And what a liar he was and is and always has been. He deserves nothing, he's had everything. He's been careless, he's forgotten. He's had a marriage, a family, a partner for so many years. In anyone's estimate that's a good, good, run.

So think of life this way, William. Don't focus on what you're losing, but what you've had. Paley said Bree left because she's redefining her world for herself every day. And maybe, you're not supposed to understand how she's surviving away from you: ego worship usually turns up blind.

He glances around this bath and bedroom. Without Bree, so much will fall away. Why will there even be a need for a curling iron in the wicker cabinet? What purpose would it have? Or why would that third shelf be filled with nylons or cosmetics? Without Bree here, this world will get small, so small.

And yet at least once before, hadn't both of them failed to be there for the other? What had rolled up then, how had it gone?

(William, remember this.)

Corey had come; all of William's worries drowned out by a newborn's cries the moment he'd pushed into the delivery room (dads not allowed in those days except see, he is also a doctor so let me by!).

Yes, yes, he'd made sure to lock glances with Bree before memorizing the ten fingers, ten toes, of a glorious son.

Until now though, he'd only considered those glances over a first child a precious confirmation of their union and never—as he is imagining now—the minutes when one part of his life with Bree *fell away so another might be claimed.*

In those final seconds of shudder, Bree had turned herself fully into the labor, and he was left on the sidelines as mere cheerleader.

The physical gap between them had been only inches then. Miles now.

Still both times seemed to reveal this lesson: a shedding comes before a grafting. Every time.

A shedding comes before a grafting. Lives change in shape and weight to let another in. And what comes up in the space in between? All this: a frantic tear of giftwrap; a lazy unwinding of limbs; a dream left to its own detouring narrative. A gash-red gap marking the spot where a budding tooth or flag or soft oyster pearl will root. Life in flux forces new definitions upon us and in return we must rise to meet what's new.

233

Maybe there had been a forfeit of sorts, a settling back into unknown spaces where they'd soon be redefined by newly birthed words: parents, mother, father. Three very sweet things.

Today, William can recall his exact thoughts in those moments when Corey was born,

These may be our last few seconds, Bree, to remember all we've been to each other. In a few minutes, I will love you differently. At times, I may even love him more. But so will you. And we will give each other permission to do this, we will. Now we both have our jobs to do. I don't exactly know how we'll move forward but trust me as I trust you, we will.

He blinks once, twice, in drunken confusion. You schmuck. You egotist, you fool. You've listened to stories of unbearable pain from patients for years and never had to come close. What babies were ever due you, what profession, what extraordinary wife?

He turns on the tap again to splash his face and the water is hot, too hot. It doesn't matter. His mind is racing with nothing more to distract than the yellow backsplash over the sink. Steamy water fogs the room and soon he can only see his eyes in the mirror's reflection.

This has been their most infertile year. The most barren landscape they've ever known.

So don't take the eye off the parched cow. Prepare for years of drought.

But also, what has he learned in all these years with Bree?

He has discovered his best self, his most unselfish parts, in the face of only uncertainty and no guarantees. Those New York treasure hunts, two babies born, two gone. Her first bout with cancer,

All these things, sweet and bitter, they are his inheritance in the marriage. So this he knows. If he has one more chance with Bree, he will make sure to catch her eye. Lead her back to that same, steady gaze they'd first exchanged over Corey's newborn self.

And that gaze is a free fall, a run up from a stumble without knowing where the next bite of air will come from, but still you go on. Ignoring all guilt, all fear.

If you can't answer it doesn't matter. I will never look away, I will not doubt. For once again, we both have our jobs to do.

Not my agenda or yours but simply a promise to trust in the next steps, whatever they may be.

And this. Yes, this.

We can't be sure how we'll move forward…

But trust me as I trust you, *we will, we will, we will.*

~37~

He's awakened by a ringing cellphone, and thank god he'd thought to plug in the charger near the nightstand.

"Hold on," he says, pushing off this night he'd been given, no dreams and an aching back. "Just hold on. Hello?"

"I'm ready to come home, William. I'm booked on an American Airlines flight that gets into LaGuardia tomorrow at 3:40. Please, will you meet me at the airport?"

-Our End-

References and Links

A triad of mental and physical disorders are addressed in this novel: Ovarian Cancer; PTSD, specifically complex PTSD; and unexplainable acts of individuals on others qualifying as child abuse.

Yet this book is fiction, and so readers might find the following lists of non-fiction books and articles valuable if they wish to learn more about any of these illnesses. They are also strongly urged to consult with medical specialists to confirm their understanding of specific symptoms or treatments.

Ovarian Cancer

"About Your Implanted Port." *Memorial Sloan Kettering Cancer Center*, August 2018, http://www.mskcc.org/cancer-care/patient-education/your-implanted-port.

"Chemotherapy for Ovarian Cancer | Intraperitoneal Chemotherapy." *American Cancer Society*, 11 April 2018, https://www.cancer.org/cancer/ovarian-cancer/treating/chemotherapy.html

Daley, Mary D., ed. "End-Stage Ovarian Cancer Symptoms | Healthfully." LIVESTRONG.COM, Leaf Group, 18 Dec. 2018, https://www.livestrong.com/article/128524-endstage-ovarian-cancer-symptoms/

Dizon, Don S., and Sparacio, Dorinda. *100 Questions & Answers About Ovarian Cancer. Third Edition.* Jones Bartlett Learning LLC., 2016.

Freedman, Jeri. *Ovarian Cancer. Current and Emerging Trends in Detection and Treatment.* The Rosen Publishing Group, Inc. 2009.

Gubar, Susan. *Memoir of a Debulked Woman.* Thorndike Press, a part of Gale, Cengage Learning, 2012.

"Ovarian Cancer-Diagnosis and Treatment." *Mayo Clinic*, https://www.mayoclinic.org/diseases-conditions/ovarian-cancer/diagnosis-treatment/drc-20375946.

Studies Exploring Connections Between Cancer and PTSD

Cancer.Net, Editorial Board. "Post-Traumatic Stress Disorder and Cancer." *Cancer.net*, Mar. 2019, https://www.cancer.net/survivorship/life-after-cancer/post traumatic-stress-disorder-and-cancer

Ellis, Janet, et al. "Are we missing PTSD in our patients with cancer? Part 1." *Canadian Oncology Nursing Journal*, vol. 29, no. 2, 1 Apr. 2019, pp. 141-146. https://www.ncbi.nim.nih.gov/pmc/articles/pmcg516338

Gradus, Jaimie L., et al. "Posttraumatic Stress Disorder and Cancer Risk: A Nationwide Cohort Study." *European Journal of Epidemiology*, vol. 30, no. 7, 9 May 2015, https://www.ncbi.nlm.nih.gov/pubmed/25957083.

Joelving, Frederik. "Many Cancer Survivors Struggle with PTSD Symptoms." *New York: Reuters Health*, Oct. 2011, http://uk.reuters.com/article/2011/10/12/health-us-cancer-ptsd-USTRE79B7FT20111012

"PTSD Linked to Increased Risk of Ovarian Cancer." *Harvard T.H. Chan School of Public Health News*, 5 Sept. 2019, https://www.hsph.harvard.edu/news/press-releases/ptsd-linked-to-increased-risk-of-ovarian-cancer/.

Tedeschi, Bob. "1 In 5 Shows PTSD Symptoms after Cancer Diagnosis, Study Finds." *STAT News*, 20 Nov. 2017, www.statnews.com/2017/11/20/ptsd-cancer-diagnosis/

Posttraumatic Stress Syndrome; Complex Posttraumatic Stress Disorder (C-PTSD)

Courtois, Christine A. *It's Not You, It's What Happened to You. Complex Trauma and Treatments.* Telemachus Press. 2014.

Croft, Harry. "Complex Posttraumatic Stress Disorder (C-PTSD) vs. Simple PTSD." *Healthy Place*, 5 June 2015, https://www.healthyplace.com/blogs/understandingcombatptsd/2015/06/complex-posttraumatic-stress-disorder-ptsd-vs-simple-ptsd

Everstine, Diana Sullivan and Everstine, Louis. *The Trauma Response: Treatment for Emotional Injury.* W.W. Norton & Company, Inc., 1993.

Flannery Jr., Raymond B. *Post-Traumatic Stress Disorder; The Victim's Guide to Healing and Recovery.* The Crossroad Publishing Company, 1999.

Herman, Judith. *Trauma and Recovery.* Basic Books, 1997.

Tull, Matthew. "What is Complex PTSD?" *Very Well Mind.* Medically reviewed by Gans, Steven. 2, Oct. 2019. https://www.verywellmind.com/what-is-complex-ptsd-2797491

Books on Child Abuse, Adult Children of Abuse, Surviving in Dysfunctional Families

Miller, Alice. *For Your Own Good.* Farrar, Straus, Giroux, 1985.

Schwartz, Richard C. *Internal Family Systems Therapy.* The Guilford Press, 1995.

Whitfield, Charles. L. *Healing the Child Within.* Health Communications, Inc., 1987.

Acknowledgments

In my long and discursive writing career, I am grateful for my association with a bevy of talented authors, editors, and publishers. I'd like to especially thank Yona Zeldis McDonough, Carlo Matos, and Sarah Sadie for not hesitating in taking a look at this book when asked. I am also grateful to those people always willing to support my creative endeavors, both professionally and personally: my dear brother Wayne Ellis, Norman, Marilyn, and Sue Goodman, Meri Franco Ezratty, Ilene Antelman, Frank Blocker, Jason Willits, Laura Weiss, Gregory Tague, Christian Nelson, Bruce Jacobs, Michele Somerville, Presley Acuna, Chris Flieller, Abe Peck, Jolie Mandelbaum, Laura DiDio, Marilyn Malcolm, the late Leo Jones, Catherine Jones, Frank Scoblete, Steve Moffic, Dennis Paul, Karl Garson, Dave Eggebrecht, the late Stephen Pollan, Mabel Wong, Chris Van Den Elzen, Bruce Jacobsen, Lonnie Carter, Kristin Kobylinski, Don Sipe, Carol Ross, Michael O'Neill, Amy Azen, Domenick Danza, Susan Angel Miller. I also want to thank the many writers I've met over the course of nearly two decades in my writer's group for their wonderful critiques of every word penned.

For the publication of this book, I am especially grateful to Christina Kubasta at the Muriel Press for accepting this novel, and the editing team of Natalie Zrinsky, Kim Zills, Bradey Resulta, Brenda Ordonez, T.J. McAdams, Molly Gross, and Kayla Gilligan for their great work on matters small and large, who gave their time and talents to this book's creation. I am also grateful to my attorney, Ellen Kozak, for her apt guidance regarding the publishing industry.

In learning about the ravages of PTSD, I have endless gratitude for the work of the late Dr. Ray Gallope, Dr. Ed Tick, Sheppard Crumrine, Michael Orban, and Dr. John Zemler.

Most of all, I am filled with endless love for Ben and Hope and their willingness to always set a place at the dinner table for any of my fictional characters dropping by.

Biography

Michele Merens is a playwright and writer whose fiction has been published in more than a dozen literary magazines and anthologies. She has also written op-ed columns for various newspapers, including *The Milwaukee Journal Sentinel*. She has been named a winner in the 2020 New York Times/Brooklyn Public Library Philosophy Op-ed Competition, and a Golden Dozen columnist by the International Society of Weekly News Editors.

In playwriting, she is a Puffin Grant recipient. Her full-length drama, *The Lion's Den*, is currently archived in the Wisconsin Veteran's Museum, Madison, WI. and her scripts/monologues have been published in print and online.

Michele holds a BA from Barnard College, where she was named a Senior Scholar in Creative Writing, and a MSJ from Northwestern University's Medill School of Journalism.

Made in the USA
Monee, IL
19 April 2021